JASMINE

The Group - Week One

M. D. MEYER

D0191095

JASMINE

Copyright © 2010 M. D. Meyer

All rights reserved. No part of this publication may be reproduced, stored in a retrieval system, or transmitted in any form or by any means—electronic, mechanical, photocopy, recording, or any other—except for brief quotations in printed reviews, without prior permission from the publisher.

Unless otherwise indicated, all Scripture quotations are taken from the Holy Bible, New International Version®. Copyright © 1973, 1978, 1984 by International Bible Society. Used by permission of Zondervan Publishing House.

Scripture quotations marked KJV are taken from the Holy Bible, King James Version, which is in the public domain.

This is a work of fiction. Names, characters, places and incidents either are the product of the author's imagination or are used fictitiously, and any resemblance to actual persons, living or dead, businesses, companies, events, or locales is entirely coincidental.

ISBN-13: 978-1-926676-87-6

Printed in Canada.

Published by Word Alive Press
131 Cordite Road, Winnipeg, MB R3W 1S1
www.wordalivepress.ca

WORD ALIVE PRESS
Just Write!

"If we are going to overcome the awful impact of abuse on our lives, we are going to have to take a courageous step and FACE THE PROBLEM."

-HOWARD JOLLY
(*Hope for the Hurting*. Rising Above, 1996)

"Surely you desire truth in the inner parts;
you teach me wisdom in the inmost place."

-DAVID, THE SHEPHERD, MUSICIAN, AND KING
(Psalm 51:6-8)

Chapter 1

A NEW BEGINNING—A FRESH START—that's what it was supposed to have been. But to Jasmine Peters, the last five months in this cold, barren north country had been less like a fresh start and more like a slow dying.

She didn't want comfort or help or "support." What she wanted was for someone to pull the plug and end her miserable existence. Close the coffin lid and let her rest in peace.

Mostly, people did leave her alone. But then, without any warning, they'd arrive, swarming around like the pesky bluebottle flies that she remembered from the summers she'd spent up here at Rabbit Lake.

Someone was knocking now on the door downstairs. Jasmine ignored them, hoping they would go away.

"Hey, Jas, where are you?"

"I'm upstairs," Jasmine yelled, knowing it was useless to pretend she hadn't heard him. Her brother-in-law, Joshua Quill, wouldn't give up so easily. He'd search through the house and keep looking until he found her.

Jasmine stayed where she was in the recliner, watching the

last few minutes of a reality show about aspiring models. She didn't want to visit with Joshua but knew it would take a keg of dynamite to deflect him from his mission.

He probably just wanted to give her the latest development in the "baby saga." Ever since Missy found out she was pregnant, that seemed to be all that either one of them could talk about.

"What if I was getting dressed or something?" Jasmine demanded as her brother-in-law reached the top step of the spiral staircase and proceeded right on into the large open loft that was Jasmine's bedroom.

Joshua waved away her question with a grin. "I'm sure you would have warned me."

Jasmine gave a loud sigh of exasperation, lowered the volume of the TV, and crossed her arms, doing her best to glare at him.

But Joshua, characteristically, didn't notice—or didn't care—what mood she was in. He was busy looking around for a place to sit, finally settling down on the spare bed that had once been Missy's when she and Jasmine had shared this large bedroom together.

He pulled off his cap, smoothed down his short black hair, and leaned towards her. "I've got some great news!" he exclaimed.

Jasmine rolled her eyes. "Ri-i-ight," she drawled, more than a little annoyed that Joshua had to sit on the spare bed. She had a desk chair and another easy chair, but they were piled high with magazines and clothes and other stuff. She'd been meaning to clean up her bedroom. But if people were just going to barge in…

"Guess who's coming home today?" Joshua continued, his dark brown eyes sparkling with delight.

Jasmine shook her head. "I don't know. And I don't care."

"Andrew!" Joshua announced with a big, happy smile—as if Jasmine had just won at Wheel of Fortune or something.

Andrew. If there was anyone in the whole world that she didn't want to see right now, it was Andrew!

Joshua looked puzzled—and then concerned. "I thought you liked him..." he began cautiously. "I mean, you used to, didn't you?"

"*Used to* is the operative term here. That means past tense—finished—over—ancient history!" Jasmine turned away, her voice trailing off as she continued, "Just like my life."

"Hey, you're really down today," Joshua said with genuine compassion in his voice. "Is your dad doing worse? I didn't see him downstairs..."

"He's fine," Jasmine said more sharply than she'd intended. "He's got a new spot to sit in now that the weather is warming up a bit." She stood, walked to the wooden railing, and pointed across the open space of the room below, through the cathedral windows towards their front yard. "He's set up a chair outside now so he can stare at the frozen lake instead of staring at the fireplace."

Joshua remained where he was and was silent for a moment. When he spoke, it was in a quiet, thoughtful voice. "Maybe we could invite Dad over for supper..."

Jasmine wrenched her eyes away from the pathetic sight of her father huddled against the wind, sitting in an old wooden deck chair that looked ready to fall apart. "He won't come," she stated flatly.

But Joshua was not so easily deterred. "Maybe it would be

better if he moved up to the lodge—even just for a little while. It might give you a break. Or maybe you could both move up there."

But Jasmine was already shaking her head. "Dad won't leave. He's made this place into some kind of a shrine to my mother. All he talks about—when he talks—is the curtains that Mom made and the flowers that she planted and where she sat and where she stood…" With a sigh, Jasmine returned to her recliner. "Dad'll never leave," she said again as Joshua also resumed his seat.

"What about you?" he asked kindly. "Would it help if you stayed at the lodge for a little while? You could spend more time with Missy and maybe help out in the kitchen sometimes if you wanted. We could always use an extra hand there."

Jasmine attempted a smile. He was trying so hard—too hard. She shook her head again. "I really don't think Dad could take care of himself here without me. And…" Jasmine hesitated. She really didn't want to hurt Joshua's feelings. "And I think that what you and Missy are doing is really commendable and I wish that I could help out in some way but…" Jasmine looked around as she continued, "I don't seem to have the energy to keep up with the things that I need to do here."

Joshua was immediately apologetic. "I don't mean that you'd have to help. We don't need help that bad." He stumbled over his words. "I mean—it would be okay if you *wanted* to." He took a deep breath and began again. "It's just that Missy—and I—we worry about you sometimes. We've been so wrapped up in our own lives—starting with your grandpa's death, I guess. And then him willing the lodge to me. We'd always talked about doing the youth program and I knew that's what he wanted me to do. But then there were all the problems with my brothers and—and your father. And then there was your mom's cancer and the operation. It was such an awesome thing for Missy to see for the first time in her life. And it was wonderful that your mom lived long enough to attend our wedding. But your dad took her death so hard—and so soon after your grandpa died. And I know he was really affected by what happened to you—"

Jasmine leapt to her feet and headed downstairs. Joshua could talk about everyone else as much as he wanted. But they were *not* going to talk about what had happened to her. It was in the past. It was going to stay in the past. It wouldn't help to talk about it. Nothing would help. Nothing would change.

Jasmine was out of breath when she reached the bottom. She paused for a moment, heard Joshua coming slowly down the stairs behind her, and moved quickly into the kitchen. She found a bag and began to fill it with cookies.

"Would you like some cookies?" She turned towards Joshua. "I just made them this morning. Maybe Missy would like some."

Jasmine pushed the bag towards him. He looked apologetic—and concerned. But Jasmine didn't want his pity. She didn't want anything from him—except to be left alone! She moved ahead of him towards the door, pulling his jacket off the hook and handing it to him.

Joshua put on his coat and boots and then took the bag of cookies from her. His eyes looked sad as he nodded in farewell.

Jasmine waited until she heard the sound of his truck fading into the distance. Then she moved from her position against the door and walked slowly forward. It was as if she were seeing the house through a visitor's eyes. She hadn't actually realized how bad it had gotten. Dirty dishes were everywhere. The stove had splashes of food on it and the floor was even worse. When had she last swept it?—Jasmine couldn't remember. Looking through to the living room, she could see empty pop cans and potato chip bags on the chairs, on the coffee table, on the floor... Maybe if she took a garbage bag...

But she was so tired—so very tired.

Maybe if she just took a little break. There were still a few cookies left. Jasmine looked in the fridge. There was still some pop left, too. And a lot of other stuff that Missy had bought for her last time she'd gone shopping. But Missy had completely ignored all the baking items on Jasmine's shopping list. Some of the fruit and vegetables that she'd purchased did look kind of good. Maybe later...

Jasmine reached for a can of pop, grabbed a handful of cookies and headed upstairs, wishing, not for the first time, that her dad would let her move the TV down to the living room. But it had been enough of a battle just to get him to okay the satellite dish.

She was still flipping through the channels, looking for something good, when another much too cheery voice called from downstairs. "Hello—anybody home?"

Sarah... Another one who just walked right on in as if she owned the place. Another one who could only talk about babies. For months, all that she'd talked about was her pregnancy and now it was all about how baby Ty did this and baby Ty did that.

Jasmine hid the remaining cookies under a magazine as her company mounted the steps and called out, "Hey, Jas, you up here?"

There was no need to answer. Soon enough, Sarah was at the top of the stairs, her baby held securely in a sling against her chest. But for once, Sarah wanted to talk about someone besides her son, Tyler.

"You'll never guess who just arrived on the plane a few minutes ago," she exclaimed. "And I bet he's on his way here right now!"

Jasmine jumped to her feet, panic-stricken. "No! He can't! He wouldn't. Sarah, please, tell him that I'm sick. Tell him that I can't see anyone. Please!"

Sarah looked at her strangely. "We are talking about the same person, aren't we?"

"Joshua already told me that Andrew was coming back," Jasmine said irritably. She threw the covers up on her bed and began to toss clothes into a laundry basket. "Doesn't he want to see his family?"

"Yes—and his friends," Sarah spoke slowly. "Do you want some help tidying up, Jasmine? Hey, are you okay?"

Jasmine touched her cheek, surprised to find a tear there. Then, without warning, it was followed by another and yet another. Jasmine swiped angrily at them.

What's the matter with me? I never cry!

"Do you want to talk about it, honey?"

"No!" Jasmine yelled. The baby startled and Jasmine immediately lowered her voice. Sarah spoke soothing words to her son before turning her attention back to Jasmine.

"I shouldn't have even moved up here." Jasmine slumped back down into the chair. "Missy thought it would help Dad. But it hasn't. If anything, he's worse. And…" Her voice trailed away.

"…It hasn't helped you much either," Sarah said, finishing the sentence for her.

Jasmine shook her head. "I'm not the person that Andrew used to know. Please, Sarah!—If you could just tell him that I'm sick or something."

"He won't be put off by that for long." Sarah smiled. "He'll want to bring you flowers or chicken soup or something. You know how Andrew is."

Yes, I do.

"And from what I hear, he's planning to live and work in Rabbit Lake. You're going to run into him eventually."

Jasmine turned away from the compassion she saw in Sarah's eyes.

A rapping sound came from below. Another visitor! "Grand Central Station here today," Jasmine muttered under her breath.

There was a pause and the person knocked on the door again.

Maybe they'll just go away…

"Do you want me to answer it?" Sarah offered.

Jasmine sighed and finally nodded. Sarah turned and hurried down the stairs. A moment later, Jasmine heard the door open and close.

She could quite clearly hear their voices.

Andrew…

She'd feared as much. Maybe—just maybe—Sarah would come through for her.

"Jasmine does live here, doesn't she? Missy said…"

"Yes, she lives here, but…" Sarah hesitated. "I was just up with her a moment ago and she told me that she wasn't feeling well."

The concern in Andrew's voice was obvious. "It's nothing serious, I hope?"

Sarah hesitated again. "No, I don't think so."

"You don't *think* so?" Andrew asked, sounding more worried than ever.

"No, it's not serious," Sarah said hurriedly. "She's fine. It's just that she's not feeling up to visitors right now."

Jasmine held her breath in the ensuing silence.

Finally, Andrew spoke again, but in a voice so quiet she had to strain to hear his words. "She doesn't want to see me," he said. "I guess I should have known. Just because we hung out together when we were kids, I guess I thought that maybe—"

"Andrew, you're jumping to conclusions—" Sarah began.

"No, I don't think so."

Jasmine heard the door close.

She waited for the sound of Sarah coming up the steps again but instead, a moment later, she heard the front door shut. Sarah had left without a word of goodbye.

SARAH HILL BUCKLED HER SON into the baby car seat and drove back home. It was still too early to pick up the girls from school. She'd been planning to spend some time with Jasmine. But after the way that girl had treated Andrew...

Sarah turned right onto the Mine Road, thankful that she had Colin's four-wheel drive truck today. The road was a bit icy in spots.

Like everyone else, she was longing for spring. "Cabin

fever"—that's what people called the late winter blues that often occurred this time of the year. Sarah shook her head. If that's what was wrong with her, Jasmine sure seemed to have a bad case of it!

As Sarah headed her vehicle towards home, she had to admit that though she was angry at Jasmine, she was even angrier at herself. She didn't appreciate being put in a position where she was forced to lie, but it really bugged her that she was the one who had to tell Andrew that Jasmine didn't want to see him. Andrew was a nice guy and didn't deserve that kind of treatment.

He'd been so excited when he'd stepped off the plane. There was quite a group of his family and friends waiting for him. His parents were planning a homecoming party for him later that evening. Andrew had been asked to wear his RCMP uniform—at least for part of the night—and he was planning to bring some pictures as well. Sarah was looking forward to hearing all about her nephew's training time with the Royal Canadian Mounted Police. Colin, her husband, was even more interested, since he hoped to recruit Andrew into the local police force. Colin had been Police Chief of Rabbit Lake for a few years now and was always on the lookout for potential new officers.

Sarah pulled into the driveway and sighed deeply, still unable to fathom the way that Jasmine had treated Andrew. The two had been best friends growing up and on into their teen years. Sarah had assumed that this strong friendship would continue—and possibly even blossom into something more.

And judging by the crushing look of disappointment she'd seen on Andrew's face, Sarah hadn't been the only one thinking along those lines.

As she opened the door of the home that had once belonged to Colin's grandfather, her husband's words of greeting turned her thoughts away from Jasmine and Andrew towards her own family.

He stepped forward to take Tyler from her. "Hey, how's my little man?"

Sarah looked lovingly at her husband as he cradled their son in the crook of his arm. Baby Ty had thick black hair like his father. "A real Indian baby," the older women in the community said. Sarah's heart had swelled up with pride as she'd heard the words. She herself was of mixed race, but her husband was full Ojibway and his parents and grandparents had always lived in this community and on this land.

"Can I fix you something to eat?" she asked him. Colin was on night-shift this week and had obviously just woken up.

"Maybe I'll wait a bit," Colin said as he continued to smile down at his son.

Sarah didn't mind that all his focus was still on the baby. They'd longed and prayed for a child for seven years before the Lord had unexpectedly blessed them with not one but three precious little children. And Colin gave each of them this kind of focused attention. People had warned them that the two older girls would be jealous, but it was impossible for them to be jealous of Colin's attention, for he lavished it liberally on each one of them. Emmeline and Verena were his special girls and his special helpers with baby Ty.

Sarah gave both her husband and her son a kiss on the cheek before moving towards the kitchen. She was sure that Colin would at least like a cup of coffee.

She'd just finished preparing a fresh pot when there was a knock on the door. Sarah called, "Come in!" and Andrew Martin stepped into their living room. He was also of mixed ancestry and had inherited the smattering of freckles across his nose and the incongruously blue-green eyes from his sandy-haired father, Bill. Andrew's hair and skin color, darker than his father's, had come from his mother, Jamie, Colin's sister.

But his smile was pure Andrew. So was his personality. He could be impetuous at times, acting before thinking, but once he'd made up his mind to do something, he was determined to follow it through. This character trait had led him, as a young kid, to carelessly hand his city friend, Michael, his snowmobile keys on the coldest night of the year. But when Andrew had realized what he'd done, he'd almost died in the process of saving his friend's life.[1]

And when his father was presumably killed in a plane crash, Andrew alone had believed it was not his father in the wreckage. He'd gone out searching for him, and he and his friend Joshua had finally found Bill, who had been shot and left for dead by a notorious criminal. The gold that had been recovered that day was still talked about and their story would be the stuff of legends for years to come.[2]

Andrew had immediately gravitated towards Colin and the baby. "So this is my new cousin," he said, smiling at Tyler and reaching down to let his finger be enclosed by the tiny little hand. "He sure has a strong grip. And he looks just like you," Andrew

---

[1] *Get Lost!*
[2] *Pilot Error*

12

said to his uncle.

Colin raised an eyebrow and grinned lopsidedly. "That's like comparing a brand new toonie with an old worn out two dollar bill."

Sarah came over to join them. "Thirty-four is not *that* old," she declared.

Colin yawned. "Night-shift always makes me feel like I'm a hundred and two." He lifted an eyebrow in Andrew's direction. "What we need is some new young bucks—guys that'll take over the night-shift duties so us old guys can stay at home with our wives and new babies."

The implication was clear and Andrew smiled slightly as he settled into the sectional adjacent to his uncle. "I *had* been thinking about staying here at Rabbit Lake—but now I'm not so sure."

Disappointment was obvious in Colin's face and in his voice. "What's happened to change your mind, Andrew?" His frown melted into a grin as he exclaimed, "You just got here!"

Andrew and Sarah exchanged brief glances as she stood to pour the coffee she'd prepared.

"I didn't say that I'd decided anything for sure," Andrew said. "I just don't know yet, that's all."

He shook his head to Sarah's offer of coffee before continuing, "I do have to stay here for a little while at least. The RCMP have asked me to work undercover on a problem you guys are having here at the Health Center."

Colin leaned forward. The intensity in his voice reflected his concern as he told Andrew about the recent thefts of highly potent drugs. Sarah lifted Tyler out of his arms as he said in a grim voice, "We think it's an inside job."

Chapter 2

"AS YOU CAN IMAGINE," Colin continued, "that's especially difficult in such a small community. We've pretty much ruled out the nurses and doctors that are here temporarily from down south. It's—uh—been going on for a while. We have some suspicions but, of course, no one wants to be the first to point a finger…"

Sarah took the quilt that she'd made before Tyler was born off the back of the rocking chair, wrapped it around her son, and sat down with him before looking up to meet Andrew's questioning glance. She gave him an amused grin. "I've been cleared as well," she said. "I haven't worked at the Health Center since we got the two girls last summer. I know about the thefts, of course. Your mom was actually the first to report the problem. She came here to talk to Colin about it." Sarah paused. "When was that, Colin? A couple of months ago at least…"

"Yeah, it started after Christmas—sometime in January," Colin answered. "I'd have to look up the exact date."

"That's like—almost three months ago," Andrew mused.

Colin sounded a little defensive. "Closer to two and a half, I'd say."

"But you're just calling in the RCMP now?"

"We thought it would be better if we could solve it locally. But things didn't work out that way." Colin stroked his chin thoughtfully. "Why did they send you?" he asked Andrew. "We called the RCMP hoping for some outside help on this."

Andrew didn't appear offended. "They wanted someone who could work undercover. A stranger would stick out like a sore thumb—scare the perpetrator away." He glanced over at Sarah and then back to Colin again. "I was told you had definite suspicions, but I was also told to go in with a clear, objective mind—to start with a clean slate, so to speak." Andrew hesitated before asking, "Is it possible that you could be wrong about the person or persons you suspect?"

Colin closed his eyes momentarily before glancing wearily up at his nephew. "I wish I was wrong. But no, I don't think I am. The RCMP are probably on the right track, though. A totally independent investigation is what we need. I only pray that you can keep an open mind and remain completely unbiased."

Now Andrew was offended. "Of course I can! I'm a trained RCMP officer. Just because I'm young—"

"It's not because you're young."

"I can be objective."

Colin sighed and rose wearily to his feet. "We will give you any assistance that you require. Keegan Littledeer is the Assistant Police Chief and you can pretty much reach one of the two of us at any hour of the day or night."

Andrew stood to go.

"We're looking forward to your big welcome home party

tonight," Sarah said, remaining in the rocking chair; Baby Ty was fast asleep in her arms.

Andrew grinned. "Mom's been talking about this party ever since she found out about my commissioning—and realized that she couldn't bring the entire population of Rabbit Lake with her to the ceremony!"

Sarah and Colin laughed. Yes, Jamie certainly would have brought the whole of Rabbit Lake with her if she could have. If they hadn't just had a baby, she and Colin would definitely have gone to Andrew's commissioning.

"She's very proud of you," Sarah said.

"We all are," Colin added.

"Thanks." Andrew said, shaking Colin's hand in farewell.

HE HAD WALKED TO THEIR HOUSE. He walked back home as well, taking the path through the bush. During the long months of training in Saskatchewan, he had often yearned to be back here on the land that he loved so well. But as he looked around, Andrew realized that he'd come home at the worst possible time of the year. The ice was still on the lake, creating a constant cold wind from the west. The snow was almost gone, but what was left of it had mixed with mud to form dirty-looking slush. There were no buds on the trees and the sky was a leaden gray, warning of more snow or perhaps a cold spring rain. Many animals were still in hibernation and none of the birds had returned yet.

Andrew thought that maybe he shouldn't have returned yet either. He'd looked forward to it for so long, but now he just had this flat, dry feeling inside.

His mom was so excited about the party tonight. He didn't want to disappoint her—or the community that had been behind him the whole way. He even had a job back here, if he wanted—Colin wouldn't have offered it to him if he wasn't sure that the Chief and Council of Rabbit Lake First Nation were in favor of it.

Opening the door of his house, Andrew felt as if he'd walked from an old black and white movie into full Technicolor. His senses were assailed with the busy chatter of friends and family and the smell of good things cooking on the stove and baking in the oven.

Andrew just stood for a moment taking in the scene before him. The kitchen and living room were combined into one with three bedrooms at the back and a bathroom off to the side. His mom was at the kitchen table, stirring some icing for a cake that looked big enough to feed a small army! Missy Quill was sitting close by her, making sandwiches. In the living room, Andrew's younger sister Kaitlyn was blowing up balloons, and off to the side his older sister Rosalee was sitting with her keyboard and conferring with Joshua Quill, who was strumming on his guitar. Rosalee's husband, Michael Rodriguez, was on the other side of the living room helping Andrew's dad pack styrofoam plates and cups into a cardboard box. They were talking about possibly needing another box.

Kaitlyn noticed him first and called out his name. A chorus of greeting followed. Andrew's eyes moved around the room again as he smiled and said, "Hey, everybody!"

And in that moment, Andrew realized that it *was* good to be home.

Kaitlyn finished tying a string to the balloon she'd just blown up, then grabbed the strings of a dozen or more balloons and held them up for him to see. Kaitlyn was sixteen now and had grown taller and slimmer since he'd been gone. "Hey, Katie," he teased. "You'd better not go outside with all those balloons. If you don't put rocks in your pockets, the wind'll just carry you away!"

She rolled her eyes dramatically and returned with, "Guess I might have to get my big hefty brother to carry them over for me then."

"Hey, I'll have you know this is all muscle!"

Katie walked up and felt his bulging bicep. "Hmm, maybe." Her voice sounded skeptical, but the twinkle in her eyes revealed her true feelings of deep affection for her big brother.

"You guys are really going to a lot of work," Andrew said.

Katie shrugged but smiled, obviously pleased that he'd noticed. "I still need some of your pictures and stuff for the display I'm making."

"And we need to know what your favorite songs are," Rosalee added. "Joshua and I have to practice and Colin wanted a list ahead of time. He's going to be our MC. Hey Mom, do you know when they're coming over?"

"After Sarah picks up the girls from school, I think."

Suddenly, Andrew felt a little overwhelmed by it all, his previous mood returning.

An MC—and songs? It wasn't like he was getting married or something!

Andrew sank down into an easy chair close to where his dad and Michael were finishing up. They'd decided to just leave some things in bags and Michael was able to carry it all out in one load to his vehicle.

"Seems like a lot of fuss," Andrew spoke gloomily.

His dad looked over, surprise and then concern in his eyes. "We thought it would be a good chance for you to see everyone," he said quietly.

"Yeah, you're right, it is. I'm sorry." Andrew attempted a smile.

Bill Martin sat down in the rocking chair beside the woodstove, pulling it a little closer to Andrew so they were almost knee to knee. Kaitlyn had moved into the kitchen, and Joshua and Rosalee were still conferring over songs while sitting side by side on the couch. Andrew's dad spoke in a low voice. "We've had three funerals this past month. It'll be nice to get together for a happy event for a change. We need something to celebrate—as a community."

Andrew smiled. "Well, I guess I don't mind being your sacrificial lamb."

"It won't be that bad," his dad protested, his face relaxing into a smile again. "At least I stopped Katie from adding your baby pictures to her display! She does want every single one of your certificates and awards, though. And Mom absolutely insists that you come dressed in full uniform."

Andrew's grin widened. "Too bad I couldn't come riding in on a horse."

His dad chuckled and patted him on the shoulder as both Kaitlyn and Rosalee called his name at the same time.

Andrew addressed his older sister's question first, advising her to just choose the songs she thought people would enjoy singing the most. Then he went with Kaitlyn into his bedroom to find the awards and pictures that she wanted for her display.

When he returned to the kitchen, his mom was just putting the finishing touches on the cake. Andrew sat down at the kitchen table, remembering when as kids they had all wanted to be the one who got to scrape out the icing bowl after his mom had finished decorating a cake, usually for one of their birthdays.

He looked up, catching her eye. She'd been watching him and anticipated his request. She smoothed some icing off the cake and added it to the little bit left on the sides of the bowl. "I suppose since you're the guest of honor..." she said with a conspiratorial smile.

Andrew grinned, picked up the knife and bowl, and tilted his chair back.

Umm!—Homemade frosting—better than candy any day.

"So is there any other way I can be of service?" he quipped, setting the well-scraped bowl back on the table.

"Actually, there is one thing I forgot to do," his mom replied. "Would you mind running to the store and getting an extra set of batteries for our camera?"

"No problem!" Andrew said, rising to his feet.

He decided to walk. It wasn't that far to the Northern Store.

He easily found the package of batteries that his mom wanted and made his way towards the checkout line.

There was only one other person in front of him. She was turned away from him slightly, gazing out the window as her purchases, mostly baking items, were being rung through. Andrew noticed her curly blond hair and thought that she must be one of the nurses or teachers from down south. She didn't look back once, even as the cashier began to bag her groceries.

Andrew thought the young woman should be making more of an effort to be friendly. After all, she had chosen to work up here …

"Your change…" the cashier said as the young woman picked up her bags at the end of the counter and began to walk away.

"Your change," the cashier said more insistently. The young woman turned back and for the first time Andrew saw her face.

Jasmine…

She didn't seem to notice him—or anyone else, for that matter. There was such a look of bleak despair in her eyes that it left Andrew speechless. And then he thought that it must not be—*it couldn't be*—Jasmine. It had only been a year. A person couldn't possibly change that much in one year!

As she took the coins and dropped them into her handbag, her eyes swept past Andrew. He heard her draw in a sharp breath, her eyes darted back towards him for an instant, and then she was gone, almost running for the door.

The thought came to Andrew that this might be his last chance—his only chance—to talk to her. He grabbed up his batteries. The cashier had bagged them and was slowly getting his change and then the receipt. "Just keep it—or give it to somebody or something. I gotta go!" Andrew said the words in a rush as he ran after Jasmine.

She was struggling to open the car door with the two bags of groceries in her hands.

"Can I help?" he asked, his tone more anxious than he'd intended.

She glanced nervously up at him. "It's okay. I can manage."

Even her voice had changed!

Andrew eased the bags out of her hands and set them down on the back seat of the little two-door Chevette.

He still could hardly believe it was really Jasmine.

She'd always been so much fun to be with. Andrew remembered her quick smile and awesome attitude. Even though she was a girl and from the city, she'd gone along with all their crazy ideas: exploring the old mine buildings, riding on his ATV, and jumping into the lake off the Tarzan swing his dad had built when they were kids. She'd spent most of her holidays at Rabbit Lake and they'd hung out as a group: Andrew, Rosalee, Michael, and Jasmine.

The sound of the car door closing suddenly pulled Andrew back into the present.

She was going to leave!

Andrew yanked open the passenger door. "No, wait! I could go with you. To help you with the groceries. To carry them inside."

Jasmine smiled wanly up at him. Tears sprang suddenly to her eyes. She swiped at her cheeks and started the engine.

Andrew got in and closed the door. Whatever was wrong, maybe he could help. He looked hesitantly over at Jasmine. If she really didn't want him there …

She was staring straight ahead. Her voice was steady but small like a child's when she spoke. "Please don't look at me."

Andrew quickly shifted his focus away from her. "Okay." He continued to look straight ahead as Jasmine backed away from the store and drove down the street towards the Mine Road.

Andrew wanted to ask what had happened. He hadn't seen

or spoken with her for over a year. He'd been surprised when she hadn't shown up for Rosalee and Michael's wedding at Christmas. Michael was her cousin besides being her friend. It wasn't as if she'd had far to travel. They'd moved back to Rabbit Lake in November—or so he'd heard.

"I missed you at the wedding—at Christmas," he ventured.

Her voice was flat and lifeless. "Dad had to go back to settle up—do some paperwork and stuff. He'd been on a leave of absence from the hospital, but then he decided he didn't ever want to go back. He turned over the care of his patients to other doctors and just walked away from it all. The closing date for the house was December 31. It was just easier to spend Christmas there. And I guess neither one of us really felt like doing much celebrating. It was still too soon after…"

Andrew hazarded a glance in her direction. Her face was set like stone—except for a tiny muscle throbbing near the corner of her eye.

"I was sorry to hear about your mother."

Jasmine flinched slightly as he spoke the words, but immediately afterwards her face solidified into a mask again.

Andrew couldn't understand it. Her mother had passed away in the fall after a lengthy illness. He had heard rumors that Jasmine's father had had a complete breakdown afterwards. He'd been a prominent neonatal surgeon but had left the hospital, sold his house, and moved permanently to the cabin he'd built at Rabbit Lake. Andrew hadn't seen him yet but was told that he'd lost a lot of weight and was on some kind of medication.

Jasmine hadn't lost weight.

Even her fingers gripping the wheel looked pudgy. If he

hadn't seen for himself, Andrew wouldn't have believed that it was possible to gain that much weight in such a short amount of time.

"Please…"

Andrew looked up and saw deep shards of pain in her eyes.

"Please don't look at me."

Andrew turned quickly away. "I'm not. I mean, I won't. I'm sorry."

Jasmine pulled over to the side of the road. "Where did you want to be dropped off?" she asked.

I'm losing her!

But I never really had her.

Jasmine was the only girl he'd ever cared for. But there'd never been anything spoken between them beyond words of friendship. She had been like some bright star that occasionally strayed into his part of the universe. But she'd never stayed for long.

"I don't want to be dropped off," Andrew said hesitantly, keeping his eyes straight ahead.

"Fine then."

Her wheels spun hard on the gravel at the side of the road as she forced the car to quickly accelerate back onto the pavement.

Andrew thought that he might be overstepping his bounds. She hadn't invited him into her car in the first place—and she had pulled over indicating that he should leave. He didn't want to push himself on her. But he couldn't just leave her to carry whatever awful burden she was struggling with alone.

Andrew wondered what kind of support she'd had from her family and friends.

"Do you see Joshua and Missy very much?" he asked.

It was a moment before she answered. "I see them sometimes," she finally said. "They've been pretty busy getting the youth program up and running."

"What about Michael and Rosalee?"

"The newlyweds? Nobody has seen much of them—besides work, of course. They were working full-time at the camp even before they were married. They have a couple of other full-time staff there, too. The program seems to be doing well. They have about ten or so people that they're working with right now."

But Andrew didn't want to talk about the youth program. "Do you see Aunt Sarah and Uncle Colin sometimes?"

"Yeah, Sarah comes over, but I don't go there. I try not to bother them. They've been pretty busy with their new baby and, of course, the two little girls that they adopted…"

"Sounds like everybody's been pretty busy," Andrew said curtly.

"What do you mean?"

They were pulling into the long graveled driveway to her house.

"It's just that it doesn't seem as if people have been very friendly or supportive towards you."

Jasmine parked the car. "They come over often enough—like this afternoon." She opened the door on her side. "I actually prefer to be alone."

Andrew moved quickly to get out of the car. He took the two grocery bags from the back seat, carried them to the house, and stood waiting for her by the door.

Jasmine looked up at him with a slow, sad smile, pulled a key out of her handbag, and unlocked the door.

He stepped in behind her. "You probably don't have to lock your door up here, you know. Especially when you just run to the store and back."

Jasmine cleared a place on the counter for him to put the groceries. She began to unpack them. "I feel safer," she said, "especially when I'm here alone. Colin finally persuaded Dad to go over to his house for supper tonight. He thinks he can talk him into going to your party later. But Dad'll never go."

"Will you?" Andrew asked quietly.

He regretted the words the moment he'd spoken them. She turned away from him, moving towards the window on the adjacent wall.

Andrew watched her standing over the sink, looking out at the bleakness of the black spring ice and the gray leaden sky.

Of course she won't go. She said she preferred to be alone. She doesn't even want me to look at her.

Andrew wondered how long this had been going on.

He looked around. The place was a mess. Why didn't someone come and help her clean? Andrew decided he would ask his mom—and Aunt Sarah, too. But maybe Jasmine had already refused their help…

"It's a bit messy."

"No," Andrew said quickly, taking his eyes off the pile of dirty dishes and looking at her, then glancing away again. "I could help—put the groceries away maybe."

"It's okay. I can manage."

She said that before. But if there was one thing that Andrew was very sure of, it was that she was *not* managing.

It was also very clear that she didn't want help of any kind.

"Um, maybe I could just hang out here for a while?"

Jasmine had been heading towards the door, obviously hoping that Andrew would follow her. She turned to face him and something of her old sense of humor appeared as she lifted her eyebrows and spoke sardonically. "You really don't know how to take a hint, do you?"

Chapter 3

ANDREW COULD FEEL THE COLOR rising in his face. "If you want me to go, I'll go."

The spark of humor left her eyes. She looked at him for a moment and then she looked past him.

Andrew was once again afraid that he had somehow pushed her too far. He was about to speak, but she was moving—past him—without seeming to even see him. As if he wasn't even there.

Andrew watched her with something akin to desperation. What was happening? He'd never seen Jasmine like this. He'd never seen anyone like this before. It was as if she was just going on autopilot. She lifted a hand, put the chocolate chips into the cupboard, then the vanilla and icing sugar and walnuts.

But though she moved stiffly and kept her face expressionless, tiny spots of color had appeared on her pale, puffy cheeks. Suddenly, she spun towards him and demanded, "Why are you here?"

Andrew scrambled for the right words to answer her. But he wasn't even sure of the question. *Why am I here in Rabbit Lake or why am I here now in this house?*

"I—I wanted to see you," he finally managed. It was at least a partial answer to both questions.

Jasmine spread out her arms on either side of her wide girth. She drew her chin up, but tears spilled out of her eyes as she stated defiantly, "So, now you've seen me."

Andrew swallowed hard. What could he say?

"Maybe—maybe we could talk, too," he suggested.

Her eyes opened wide, her face twisted with emotion, and for a moment Andrew didn't know if she was going to laugh or cry. Maybe she didn't know either. But some of the rigidity was gone from her body as she walked over to an island counter in the middle of the kitchen. By the time she had lifted herself up onto one of the barstools, her features had softened into a tremulous smile.

Cautiously, Andrew eased down onto the stool opposite her.

"So, how was the RCMP training?" she asked in a voice that was meant to be cheery.

She's trying so hard. Andrew concentrated on the question and not on the tremor in her voice. She was trying to make conversation. She had asked him a question.

"Lonely," he admitted.

Funny, he'd never told anyone else that.

"Didn't you make friends?" she asked, all her attention on him now.

Andrew nodded thoughtfully. "Yes, I think so. But it took a while." He hesitated, trying to find the words to explain what he himself barely understood. "When you first get there, everyone's trying to find their place." He grinned. "Their spot on the food chain."

Her eyes widened and Andrew quickly amended, "Well, maybe it's not quite that bad. But there was a lot of competition. And there were definite cliques that formed. I didn't really fit any of them."

"Andrew, you're one of the friendliest, most confident people that I know," Jasmine protested.

He smiled his thanks before continuing, "There were a number of other Aboriginal cadets there and we were given specialized training to prepare us for the unique situations we might find in isolated northern communities." Andrew shifted in his seat. "The problem is that I don't really look very Native. My skin and hair are not as dark as most and my eyes…" His voice trailed off.

"I like your eyes," Jasmine spoke defensively.

Andrew felt the color rising in his cheeks. "Yeah, well, anyways…"

Jasmine leaned towards him. "People ostracized you because of your eye color!"

She sounded almost angry on his behalf. Andrew felt a drumbeat of joy—a steady rhythm that gained in strength even as he quickly amended his words. "It wasn't that bad really. And once people got to know me… Now, the drill sergeant…" Andrew grimaced. "He was just nasty. But at least he showed no partiality. Every one of us at one time or another had to hit the floor and give him twenty or thirty or forty!" He could see the question in Jasmine's eyes. "Push-ups," he said grimly. "And not those sissy girl kind either."

"And what exactly are you implying?" she demanded haughtily. "That girls can't do push-ups as well as guys? I bet I could do more than—" Jasmine broke off suddenly.

They both realized that she probably couldn't even do one push-up in her present condition. Andrew scrambled around in his mind for a new topic.

But Jasmine was standing to her feet. "I have a new recipe for brownies. You put chocolate chips into the batter…"

She was waiting for some response from him. Andrew spoke hesitantly, "Sounds good."

Her smile was one of gratitude. She reached into a cupboard for a mixing bowl and a measuring cup.

Andrew felt like kicking himself. It was like giving an alcoholic permission to drink in your presence. For surely this was the explanation of her drastic weight gain—it was like she was drowning her sorrows—not in alcohol, but in food. Andrew prayed silently that God would somehow give him the wisdom he needed to say and do the right things. He desperately wanted to help Jasmine, not hurt her further.

Maybe he could talk her into going with him to the Community Center. Or maybe she would at least send the brownies with him when he went.

"There's eggs in the fridge. You can crack them into here." Jasmine handed him a small ceramic bowl. "Unless, of course, you think it's a sissy girl thing to help in the kitchen," she added with an impish grin.

Andrew smiled back at her. "I won't say I'm an expert," he admitted. "But I am willing to learn."

They worked together, Andrew following her instructions, until the brownies were ready to be put into the oven. Then

Andrew began to fill the sink with hot soapy water.

"Oh, you don't have to do those," Jasmine said.

Andrew laughed. "The very few times that I did do cooking or baking at home, my mom always insisted that I clean up the mess that I'd made."

"I can do it later."

Andrew shrugged. "I really don't mind."

She was sitting down again. Andrew thought she looked tired. Maybe she was sick or something. If all she ate were sweets and junk food...

"Do you take vitamins?" he asked.

"What!" Jasmine exclaimed in an offended tone.

"I mean, it's kind of hard to get fresh fruit and stuff up here this time of year." Andrew backpedaled as fast as he could. "It's just that you seem a little tired."

"I'm fine," Jasmine declared, standing to her feet. "I can do the dishes. I just didn't want to do them right now, that's all."

Andrew remained where he was. The sink was full. He slid some plates into the water. They'd have to soak a bit anyway; they must have been from the day before, or possibly two or three days ago.

"Andrew Martin! I didn't invite you over here to do my dishes!"

Andrew just grinned at her. She hadn't invited him over at all!

He filled the other sink and dipped a washed cup into the clear, hot water. "Do you have a dish drainer?" he asked.

"It's under the sink." She moved to get it for him.

"Just relax. I can get it." Andrew pulled the drainer out and set it on the counter. Jasmine continued to hover uncertainly. "Sit! Sit!" he ordered, waving his hands dramatically. "You think I don't know how to do dishes now, or what?"

She smiled at his feigned indignation and sat down again.

"Now, I've told you about me," Andrew said cheerfully as he set another cup on the drain board. "What's been happening with you?"

The silence lengthened between them and Andrew hazarded a glance at her. Jasmine had that frozen look again—staring out at the dark, silent lake. "It's been so cold," she said.

Andrew turned to face her. "It will get warmer," he spoke gently. "Sometimes, it seems as if the winters up here last forever. But believe me, another month or two and you'll be complaining about the heat."

Jasmine pulled out of her reverie and looked at him. "I won't complain about the heat." She made it sound like a vow.

Andrew nodded solemnly. "So did you get some good books read this past winter?" he asked, turning back to the dishes.

"Mostly just TV," Jasmine replied in a quiet voice.

Andrew glanced at her again and inquired, "Any favorite shows?"

Jasmine smiled and began to tell him about a series that she liked a lot. Andrew listened and continued to work his way through the dishes that had littered the counters and stove. Occasionally, Jasmine made a mild protest, but Andrew just smiled and asked her about the other shows that she'd been watching. As they talked, Andrew moved into the living room, gathering up cups and bowls from the coffee table and end tables. He picked up a few candy wrappers and potato chip bags as well, unobtrusively dropping them into the garbage as he carried the dirty dishes to the sink.

Andrew had just begun washing the top of the stove when the timer went off, signaling that the brownies were done. Jasmine slid off the stool, got some potholders, and took the pan out of the oven.

"I should make some icing."

"They're probably really good, even without icing," Andrew said quickly.

Jasmine arched an eyebrow in his direction. "You just don't want to have to do any more dishes," she teased.

Andrew grinned at her, then finished wiping off the stove. When he was done, he emptied the dirty dishwater and asked Jasmine if she had a drying towel.

"I'm a little behind on the wash," she said apologetically. "Maybe we could just let them air-dry." She reached up for a plate and began to cut the still warm brownies.

"Well, I guess we've earned a break," she said, opening the fridge door. "What would you like to drink? We have some Pepsi, Sprite, juice or milk."

"Milk or juice would be fine," Andrew replied, his thoughts still on Jasmine and her nutritional needs.

She smiled at him and took milk and orange juice out, setting both on the island counter. She placed a glass on either side with the brownies in the middle and sat down, inviting Andrew to join her.

He was just about to pour some juice when there was a perfunctory knock on the door and a voice called out.

It was Andrew's mother. "What in the world are you doing

here?" she demanded.

Andrew turned, and in that instant remembered that he had been sent to buy batteries and that he had a party to go to—one for which he was the guest of honor. Andrew glanced down at his watch and immediately jumped off the stool. "Oh, no!"

"We've been looking everywhere for him!" Jamie spoke in an exasperated voice. "Didn't you know there was going to be a celebration in his honor tonight? Couldn't you have planned—*this*—for some other time?"

His mom was yelling at Jasmine! That was the last thing she needed.

"It was my idea," Andrew spoke quickly. "*I* was the one who invited myself in. *I* was the one who forgot about the time."

Jasmine was slowly removing the items from the island counter. Andrew watched helplessly as she seemed to shut down emotionally, her actions and movements once more as if on autopilot.

He turned towards his mother. "If you could just give me a minute—please. Nothing up here starts on time anyways. And people will be okay to just visit with each other for a while until I get there."

His mom shook her head but smiled indulgently at him. "Okay, I'll be out in the car. Just don't take too long."

She left, shutting the door behind her.

As Andrew watched Jasmine put first the juice and then the milk in the fridge, he felt a rush of emotion. For that little space of time, he'd had her. They'd had each other. But he'd lost her again.

It was unbearable.

"Jasmine…"

She hadn't heard him. His voice had betrayed him—the pain in his heart squeezing his throat closed so the word was a bare whisper.

But she had heard him. He saw it in her eyes as she turned slowly to face him. There was a sadness there and resignation.

"It wouldn't work."

She said it with such finality!

"Jasmine…" His voice was betraying him again. He didn't want to convey this much emotion!

He took a deep breath and moved across the room to be closer to her. "I just want to visit you." He spoke each word carefully. "We can just talk. That's all." Now he sounded like he was begging! Maybe he was…

But she was smiling now—just a little.

He felt breathless, as if he'd just run a race. He wanted to collapse with relief, but somehow managed instead to return her smile.

"Tomorrow?" he asked tentatively.

Some of the sadness returned to her eyes, but she nodded her assent.

Andrew wanted to whoop and dance around. But he knew to walk slowly and carefully. He was holding a delicate, precious thing—her love and her trust for him.

"Tomorrow, then. I'll see you tomorrow. Maybe I could come over in the afternoon—or maybe in the morning—if that'd be okay…"

A blast of a car horn sounded.

Jasmine laughed. "Go!" She took him by the shoulders and

Andrew allowed himself to be turned towards the door. She gave him a little shove. "Before your mother has my head on a platter!"

Andrew hurried out to the car, apologizing to his mom even before he was seated. As they drove away, she talked to him about the party, telling him that his uniform was in the back, that he needed to put it on as soon as they got there ... Andrew heard her and must have responded appropriately. But part of his mind and all of his heart was back with Jasmine. She'd laughed! Andrew had forgotten how much he loved the sound of her laughter ...

"YOU STILL WITH US, BUDDY?"

Andrew glanced from Michael to Joshua and then back to Michael again, trying desperately to remember the current topic of conversation. Something about the NHL playoffs ...

"Yeah, sure." He met Michael's amused grin with a defiant look. "You guys were just talking about how Jonathan Cheechoo scored the winning goal and—"

Both of his friends burst out laughing.

"What's so funny?" he demanded.

Michael was laughing so hard he couldn't speak.

"That was what we were talking about a good five or ten minutes ago," Joshua explained.

"Where you been, man?" Michael jabbed him in the ribs.

Andrew took a sip of punch and tried to think of a way to shift the topic—away from himself.

But Michael was having too much fun to stop now. "I bet you found a girlfriend out there in Saskatchewan—some pretty little farmer's daughter. She went all gaga over your spiffy little police costume."

Andrew gritted his teeth and fumed. *It isn't a costume; it's my uniform!*

Andrew was proud to wear every piece of it, from the wide brimmed beige hat, the scarlet coat with the black belt, all the way down to the black pants with the yellow stripe on the side that tucked into his knee-high polished black boots. He was a member of one of the most recognized and elite police forces in the world.

Andrew's glare only seemed to fuel the fire. "Yeah, yeah, I can tell by the look on your face. I'm right, aren't I?" Michael poked him in the ribs again. "C'mon, admit it. You got yourself a girlfriend, right?"

Andrew struck out hard against Michael's arm—harder than he'd intended.

Michael backed away. "Alright, alright. Chill!" He put his arms up in a gesture of surrender.

Andrew shook his head. "I'm sorry, Mike."

"I didn't mean no offense, man."

Andrew sighed. "Yeah, I know," he said. Michael was just being Michael. It was how he was and always would be.

Joshua stood to his feet. "Hey, you want a piece of cake or something?"

Andrew shook his head.

He wondered how many of the brownies Jasmine had eaten after he'd left…

Chapter 4

JASMINE'S FATHER ARRIVED HOME shortly after Andrew left. Colin spoke a few words to Jasmine but her father didn't say a word—just walked into his bedroom and shut the door.

Colin didn't stay long. He invited her to the party but she just shook her head, no. She'd already declined once today. This time was easier.

Jasmine moved the brownies from one counter to the other and thought again about making icing for them. But Andrew didn't seem to like icing that much. And she should save some for him.

Jasmine opened the cupboard to get another plate to divide up the brownies. But she didn't really want to dirty another plate. Not after Andrew had done up all the dishes for her.

With sudden decision, Jasmine took the whole plate of brownies and a couple of cans of pop, and headed upstairs to her room.

She flipped through channel after channel. As usual, they were running the same shows on different stations in the same time slot. She'd never figured out the sense of that. Did they really think that the whole world would want to sit down at the same time to watch the same show? What was the point of having lots of different channels?

Maybe she should have gone to Andrew's party. It was a big deal what he'd done—completing his RCMP training. She hadn't gone beyond high school—probably never would now.

Jasmine sighed as she stopped at a popular evening sitcom. It was actually more like a soap opera. You could watch one show per month and follow the simple plotline that was supposed to keep the audience hooked for the entire season.

Brain candy. That's what Sarah had called the show when she'd come over one evening while it was on.

Jasmine looked down at the plate of brownies, surprised that they were still all there. Normally, she would have eaten most of them without noticing it. But she hadn't touched even one since her and Andrew had baked them.

Jasmine flipped the channel, heard a "joke," and listened as the TV audience burst into laughter. Jasmine wondered what was so funny about what had been said. *The definition for a Hispanic woman is: single mom.* It didn't seem more acceptable or funnier because a Hispanic woman had said it.

She looked down at the brownies again.

What's happened to me?

This time last year, she'd been looking forward to her high school graduation. It had been a wonderful time. At the awards ceremony, she'd been called up again and again amidst applause from the school and family and friends. Besides doing well in scholastics, she'd excelled in sports, music, and drama. And she'd had tons of friends. She'd been president of her church youth group her last year of high school and was part of the worship team Sunday mornings.

She hadn't once touched her guitar—not since...

Jasmine took a bite from one of the brownies. It tasted like cardboard. The TV audience laughed again. Jasmine changed the channel. Back to the sitcom.

"Arghhh!" Jasmine threw the brownies at the TV as her teeth-gritting howl of rage filled the room. The plate shattered, sending shards of glass across the floor.

She was losing it. She was *really* losing it.

Jasmine started to pick up the pieces of glass, but her hands were trembling so much that she decided to wait and clean it up later.

Her fingers reached out for one of the brownies. It still looked okay...

IT SNOWED THAT NIGHT and all the next morning. When Jasmine looked out her window, she could see nothing except a moving screen of snowflakes. A cold silent world inside and out.

Her father sat by the fireplace, but the fire had long since died. He was staring out at the snow.

What does he see?

Jasmine wished, not for the first time, that he would agree to having an oil furnace installed. The house had an outdoor woodstove that needed to be "fed" at least twice a day. Her father never seemed to notice if the house was too hot or too cold, so the job of putting wood into the firebox usually fell on her.

Not wanting to bother with the struggle of putting her own

boots on, Jasmine slipped on her father's larger ones. She wore his coat as well. Actually, most of the clothes she wore these days were her father's and he was wearing some of her castoff t-shirts that were now too small for her. Joshua had given him a couple pairs of pants. Her dad had dropped several sizes but refused to buy any new clothes for himself.

Jasmine pulled open the door. Snow blew in as she stepped outside. She was thankful at least that Joshua and Colin had provided them with a winter's supply of wood, cut and stacked by the outdoor woodstove.

Jasmine walked out into what felt like a blizzard. The wind was whipping off the lake, driving the snow at her and over her and around her. As soon as she stepped away from the house, Jasmine felt swallowed up in the swirling maelstrom. Quickly she looked back to be sure that she could still see the house. It was like being in a black and white picture—the house a barely discernable mass amid the sea of white.

With each step, she glanced back again. Yes, she could still see it. And she was going in the right direction. The woodstove was up ahead.

Jasmine looked back once more, out of habit now. She felt fairly confident that she could find her way back after loading up the stove.

Suddenly, out of the swirling snow, another shape loomed. Moving closer towards her…

He had some kind of large round object in his hand. His face was a dark blur.

Fear drove all conscious thought from her mind. Jasmine turned and ran.

She glanced back only once. He was yelling and waving his arms. But the wind whipping around them drove the sound of his voice far away.

The huge boots of her father's were slowing her down— causing her to stumble. She fell heavily forward.

She struggled to rise. She had to escape!

She couldn't go through that again. Not again…

Suddenly his hand was on her shoulder pulling her off balance. Pulling her downward. Like before…

She lashed out with all her remaining strength. But she was striking thick padding and trying to scratch and gouge through a face mask.

It's me, Jasmine. It's me.

It took time for the voice to penetrate through the nightmare of her flashback.

The universe shifted. Time and space realigned.

"Jasmine, don't be scared. It's just me, Andrew."

She crumpled forward, her strength gone.

She was safe.

"I'm sorry that I scared you. I had to grab you. You were running toward the lake. The ice is thin. I was afraid…"

She lifted her head. He'd pulled the face mask up.

"No one answered when I knocked on the door. Your dad's coat and boots were gone. I thought maybe he was outside, getting wood. It was really cold in your house. I thought I would help your dad." Andrew paused for breath, then continued in a gentle voice. "Jasmine, I'm so sorry. I didn't mean to scare you."

She tried to speak—to tell him she was okay now. But her voice broke on the first syllable. The compassion in his eyes…

"It's okay to cry. It's okay… It's okay."

The wind and snow continued to blow around them. But gradually the storm within her subsided.

Jasmine couldn't remember the last time she had cried so hard. Yes, now she could. The day that it had happened. She'd told Joshua. His tears on her behalf had loosened the floodgates and she had sobbed uncontrollably—right there in the emergency room.

"Let me help you up. We'll get you inside out of this wind. I'll put the wood in later."

Andrew helped her to stand, then let go of her. But Jasmine grabbed onto his arms again, desperate for human contact. When he'd let her go, she'd felt cut adrift, a tiny boat on a huge, windy lake.

Andrew seemed to understand. He put his arm around her and they slowly made their way back to the house together.

Jasmine felt weak and vulnerable. All her defenses had crumbled.

They would need to be rebuilt. And that would take time.

He opened the door for her and steadied her as she stepped out of her boots. He put a hand on the counter to brace himself as he removed his own heavy snowmobile boots. Jasmine fumbled with the zipper on her dad's oversized parka. Her hands were trembling.

"You weren't wearing mitts," Andrew chided.

Jasmine watched as he set his mitts and facemask beside a shiny black snowmobile helmet—the large round object. *How could she have perceived it as a weapon?*

The zipper stuck at the bottom. The metal was cold. Her

hands were cold.

Andrew pulled the zipper loose and helped her remove her coat.

"I forgot…"

Andrew turned back from hanging up their coats. His voice was gentle. "What did you say?"

Her throat burned and it was an effort to speak. *How long had she been crying?*

"Mitts…" she spoke hoarsely. "I forgot them."

He was staring at her with deep kindness in his eyes. But she didn't want to be the target of such an intense gaze.

Jasmine swallowed, trying to moisten her throat a little. "I'm okay," she said in what she hoped was a strong voice. She took a step forward, away from him.

But when he put his arm around her, she felt grateful.

"Just sit over here. I'll get a fire going for you and your dad, and then I'll put some wood on outside."

He led her to the corner of the couch closest to the fireplace. There was a wool blanket draped over the back of it. Andrew pulled the opposite corner off and handed it to Jasmine and she huddled under the blanket as Andrew bent over the fire and began to set the logs in place.

"Do I know you?"

His voice startled her. But she'd known, at least peripherally, that her father was there. How had they come to this point—where they so much ignored each other as to hardly notice if the other person was present or not?

"Yes. I'm Andrew—Andrew Martin."

Jasmine stared at her father. It *was* possible that he hadn't seen Andrew for a few years, or at least not noticed him especially.

Her father was nodding thoughtfully. "Jamie's son." He looked at Andrew intently. "You've grown."

No one would have blamed him if he'd burst out laughing, but instead Andrew very seriously answered, "Yes," and after a moment, turned back to light the fire.

Jasmine, watching him, thought what an incredibly nice guy he was. Too nice to have someone hurt him, that was for sure.

Andrew stood to his feet. Flames were beginning to curl up and around the wood. "That's good dry Jack Pine," he said. "We should have a nice hot fire in a few minutes."

He tucked the blanket in around her feet, but Jasmine was still shivering. "You need something hot to drink," he said. "Would you like tea or coffee or maybe hot chocolate—if you have any?"

The double question confused her and the simple decision of what to drink seemed overwhelming. "I don't know," she finally answered.

Andrew looked at her father, but it was obvious that he was lost in his own world once again, staring out at the still falling snow.

Andrew turned back to Jasmine and said in a cheerful voice, "My mom used to always say there was nothing like a cup of hot chocolate to warm you up on a cold winter's day."

Jasmine smiled up at him. "Hot chocolate sounds good."

As he headed towards the kitchen, Jasmine turned to look at the fire. As Andrew had predicted, the Jack Pine was burning well. She could feel the heat of it already. And the hot chocolate he brought her a moment later was thick and rich. Jasmine took a sip. It tasted delicious and it was wonderfully hot as well.

Andrew set a cup of hot chocolate on the table beside Jasmine's father. Doctor Peters didn't move or acknowledge his presence in any way. Andrew hesitated and seemed about to speak.

"Just leave it there," Jasmine spoke wearily. "He'll drink it eventually."

Andrew nodded and moved away.

Jasmine's father slowly turned his eyes away from the window and focused them briefly on her. Then, still without speaking, he stood to his feet, walked into his bedroom, and shut the door.

Jasmine felt sorrow rising up from deep within, pressing against her throat, threatening to once again crumble her fragile defense.

"I should go soon," Andrew said, sitting down beside her.

Jasmine grasped his arm. "No!"

Some of her hot chocolate spilled on the blanket. Andrew looked at it and then at her. "I have to go to work," he said slowly and carefully.

Jasmine tried to control the rising panic. *What was wrong with her anyway?* "You have a job already? You just got here."

"I'll stay a while longer," Andrew said gently. She felt him touch the hand that was still gripping his arm and realized that she was holding on much too tightly. She relaxed her grip but didn't completely let go. Andrew continued to rest his hand on hers.

"It's not actually a job," he said. "It's an investigation I'm conducting—on assignment from the RCMP. But I do need to get started on it. I've been given a temporary desk down at the station."

Jasmine relaxed her grip a little more. He had to go to work. He had a job to do. She had to let him go.

She leaned forward, ready to rise to her feet.

"No, no, it's okay." Andrew took her hand off his arm and held it for an instant before releasing it. "Your hands are still cold," he said, lifting the cover that had fallen and setting it on top of her again. "You stay here and get warm while I go fill up the woodstove."

Jasmine smiled up at him, grateful for his kind words and actions.

She wasn't surprised when he came back in again after he'd done the wood, but she was a little startled when Andrew asked her when she'd last eaten. Jasmine didn't tell him about the brownies specifically, but did admit to a late night snack.

But Andrew was more concerned about the fact that she hadn't had either breakfast or lunch and he insisted upon making some food for her before he left.

He headed towards the kitchen, refusing her offer to help. But as he worked, he called out occasionally asking her about her food preferences.

"Be sure to make enough for yourself as well," Jasmine told him.

Andrew came into the living room then and quietly asked about her father.

Jasmine told him that she always waited until her dad emerged from the bedroom before preparing any food for him.

He never responded when she knocked on the door and sometimes he'd be in there for several hours at a time. But when he was out of his room and food was placed in front of him, he usually ate at least a little.

"That must be very difficult for you," Andrew said, sitting down beside her.

Jasmine shrugged and smiled faintly. It was her life—and certainly not the most difficult part of it.

"Jasmine…" Andrew looked at her intently. "When you were afraid of me—outside…"

She didn't want to talk about it. Jasmine shook her head slightly and looked away.

"I have to ask you this," Andrew persisted. "Out there—did you think that—that I was your father?"

"No!" she cried out, aghast. *How could he even think such a thing?*

"I'm sorry," he said sincerely. "I don't really know him that well. I just wondered, that's all."

Andrew was the one to look away now. "Can you—" He glanced back at her and then away again. "Can you tell me—what happened?"

Jasmine felt as if her chest was being crushed—all of her breath squeezed out of her.

The silence lengthened between them.

Andrew stood to go back to the kitchen and Jasmine spoke the words in one quick breath. "I was raped."

Chapter 5

SHE HEARD HIM GROAN AS IF IN PAIN and felt him sink back down onto the couch beside her.

Jasmine looked at him. Andrew was bent over, his head bowed.

She wanted to tell him that it was okay—that she was mostly over it.

And she wanted to tell him that he hadn't heard the worst yet.

But she couldn't find any words to say at all.

Finally he raised his head and asked, "When?"

Jasmine smiled wanly. "Eight months, two days and…" She looked at her watch. "…About five hours."

Andrew stared at her. When he spoke again, his voice was a hoarse whisper. "Who?"

"They never found him."

She could see the anger tightening Andrew's neck, rising in his face, and flashing out of his eyes.

"It was better, really," she said quickly. "There was so much else going on. This—what I just told you about—it happened on the same day that my sister and mom had their eye transplant. My sister saw for the very first time in her life. My mom had wanted her to be able to see on her wedding day. And she had wanted them to have their wedding before she died. So Missy and Josh got married a week after... after it all happened. And then my mom died just eighteen days after that. And then there was the funeral. And Dad sold our house. Then he left his medical practice and we moved up here."

Andrew had moved from anger to despair. "No one helped you."

"Joshua—" Jasmine began in his defense.

"*Joshua!*" Andrew's voice held an edge again. "Joshua was busy getting married and then he moved up here and started the youth program."

"They—Missy and Joshua—they bring up the subject sometimes—"

"When it fits their schedule. Where were they when you needed them?"

"Our—our mother was dying."

Tears filled Andrew's eyes and thickened his voice. "So were you."

Jasmine shook her head and tried to smile. She felt this urge to comfort and reassure him. To tell him it wasn't so bad. To take away some of the pain that she saw in his eyes.

But it was her pain that he was bearing—her load that he was sharing.

It made her think of the time when she'd gone hiking in the mountains with her family. She'd had terrible cramps that day but had been determined to continue the climb anyway. When they'd stopped for lunch, her dad had insisted upon reshuffling the weight; he'd taken all the heavy stuff out of her bag and put it into his, shifting some of the lighter stuff from his bag into hers. It had made such a difference! She still hadn't felt too well and she had hated to see her dad carrying such a heavy load, but to this day, his act of kindness remained etched in her mind.

Andrew rose heavily to his feet. "I was making your lunch."

"I don't want you to miss work," Jasmine protested.

Andrew smiled wanly. "I don't have any fixed hours and I didn't have lunch yet either. Besides, I'll probably be doing some surveillance work late tonight."

"You're trying to catch a criminal—by yourself?"

Andrew's eyebrow shot up. "You don't sound too confident in my abilities."

"That's not what I meant. It's just that…"

Andrew's face relaxed into a grin. "I'll have backup if I need it." He walked over to the fireplace, stooped down, and put two more logs on. "Warm enough?" he asked, rising to his feet again.

Jasmine nodded and Andrew made his way back into the kitchen.

The meal he cooked was the very best that Jasmine ever remembered tasting. Andrew had gone all out making an omelet with ham, cheese, tomatoes, mushrooms, green peppers, and onions. He'd also prepared toast and slices of fresh fruit and had served it all with a tall glass of milk and a cup of coffee for each of them.

They ate mostly in silence. Jasmine knew that Andrew was probably still thinking about what they'd talked about. But she was grateful to him for not bringing it up again. And it was just nice being with him—and eating a meal together.

After he left, Jasmine pulled the blanket up around her shoulders, put her head on the arm of the couch, and within minutes had fallen fast asleep.

ANDREW'S MIND WAS IN A WHIRL and he could hardly concentrate on the job at hand. He wanted desperately to be able to help Jasmine in some way. But he wasn't a trained counselor and didn't know the first place to begin.

And he had an assignment—an important one—and his first.

He'd put in a bit of legwork after leaving Jasmine's house. Now he was trying to work through some of the information that he'd accumulated. They'd lent him a desk and a computer to work on at the Rabbit Lake police station. He'd typed in what he had gleaned so far and was thinking about one of his academy instructor's favorite themes—ALFAP—Always Look For A Pattern.

He'd assembled a list of the stolen drugs and the times and dates when they had been reported missing. There *was* a definite pattern there—the same drugs taken each time at three-week intervals. And their loss was always discovered in the morning. But then it did make sense that the thief would come at night.

Andrew had borrowed an up-to-date Physician's Desk Reference from his mom, the head nurse at the Rabbit Lake Health Center, and had discussed each of the stolen drug's properties with her. They were of two main drug classes— amphetamines and barbiturates—basically uppers and downers. They were powerful habit-forming drugs with great potential for harm if they fell into the wrong hands.

Andrew's mother did say that, in this case, she thought Andrew could probably rule out any kind of drug ring. She said that they had probably been stolen for strictly personal use. But she refused to even give a hint of whom she suspected and Andrew, judging by her agitated manner, thought that she must have a pretty good idea who it was and that this person was someone she knew well and personally cared about.

As Andrew typed up a report of what he had so far and made a list of what he needed to do next, he thought about just how difficult this assignment was turning out to be. The community had requested help from the RCMP because they wanted somebody from the outside to handle a potentially sticky situation. Andrew *wasn't* from the outside. He had been born and raised in Rabbit Lake.

He mentioned this to his superior when he e-mailed his preliminary report. But she sent a message back telling him that he was doing a fine job and that he should continue with the investigation as planned.

Andrew sighed and glanced at his watch. Almost eight o'clock. He stood up, poured a fresh cup of coffee, and went outside to get a breath of fresh air.

From where he stood on the station's steps, he could see much of the community that was built around the lake that bore its name. Spirals of smoke rose from the houses and disappeared into the low hanging clouds in the darkening sky. Andrew looked to the north and picked out the landmark of the old headframe of Goldrock Mine and from there worked back to where he knew the house on Sandy Point would be. The lake was white now with freshly fallen snow, and the slightly darker color of smoke coming from the outdoor woodstove at Jasmine's house was just barely discernable in the distance.

Suddenly Andrew felt an overwhelming need to talk to her.

He pulled out his cell phone. He knew her number by heart. He'd almost called her the day before—when she hadn't been there at the airport with everyone else.

He'd been pretty disappointed at first and then he'd told himself that he really had no reason to expect her there. He'd finally asked Missy about her and she'd given him Jasmine's number. He'd almost called once or twice, but in the end he'd decided it might be better to just drop in at her house instead.

But things were different now. He was sure that she would want to talk to him. Or at least he hoped…

Andrew was about to hang up after the third ring when Jasmine's voice came on the line. She sounded a little sleepy.

"Uh, I'm sorry, did I wake you?"

"Andrew!" The delight in her voice was obvious. "No, don't worry. I was already awake. But I'd been sleeping almost since the time you left." She laughed. "What'd you put in that hot chocolate?"

"Nothing—honest!" he protested.

"Well, I guess I was just really tired and didn't know it. Hey, have you eaten supper yet? I was just thinking about fixing something to eat. Would you like to come over?"

Andrew just barely restrained a whoop of joy. "I'm on my way!"

He walked back into the station, turned off his computer, slid a hard copy of his report into a drawer and locked it, taking the key with him.

Colin had given him his old Ford truck to drive around. It was actually in pretty good condition, even though it was over ten years old. It had an extended cab and four-wheel drive and handled well in ice and snow. Andrew made good time getting to Jasmine's house in less than five minutes.

She had a smile on her face when she answered the door. It was so good to see her smiling again! It lit up her whole face. She'd done something different with her hair too, and she had on a bright yellow top.

"You look nice," he said, feeling suddenly shy and awkward.

"And you look awesome!" she exclaimed.

Andrew glanced down at his RCMP uniform, realizing that it was the first time Jasmine had seen him wearing it. "Thanks," he said, feeling his chest swell with pride as she gazed admiringly at him.

Jasmine carefully hung up his coat when he handed it to her. Andrew set his hat and gloves on a shelf, then slipped off his boots.

Jasmine was beaming at him. "Do you like spaghetti?"

"Love it!" Andrew responded cheerfully.

"It's only sauce from a jar, but it has mushrooms."

"Sounds great," Andrew assured her.

She remembered that he liked mushrooms!

"And I have cheese we can grate on top of it. And would you like a salad?"

Andrew offered to help and they were soon working side by side in the kitchen.

There was a small drop-leaf table up against the wall between the kitchen and living room. Jasmine pulled it out and set it with placemats and napkins. Andrew wished suddenly that he had brought some flowers or something—a difficult thing to do at the spur of the moment this time of the year. Maybe if somebody was flying in from down south, he could ask them…

"Hey," Jasmine's voice held a teasing quality. "Where were you just now?"

Andrew grinned sheepishly. "Uh, Dryden possibly—or Kenora." They were the closest larger towns that would have florist shops.

Jasmine laughed. "Well, I think everything's ready," she said.

There was a third plate set. Jasmine went over to her father's chair by the fire to invite him to join them.

The answer must have been no, or perhaps there had been no answer at all. Some of Jasmine's joy seemed to have dissipated as she prepared a plate of food for her father and set it down with a glass of water on the table beside him.

Andrew waited for her to sit down. Jasmine chose a seat facing away from the living room. Andrew had a clear view of Doctor Peters. He hadn't made a move to touch the food. It was as if she hadn't even placed it there. Andrew felt some anger towards the man and then he just felt pity. Doctor Peters was a shadow of what he had been—physically and emotionally. He seemed to have even shrunk in size. Andrew couldn't imagine what it must be like to lose as much as this man had—his wife, his home, his career. But he seemed to be cutting himself off from the rest of the human race. And he was hurting Jasmine—and she'd been hurt enough already.

"Andrew…"

The imploring tone in her voice drew his attention back to her and to the meal she had prepared. The food was getting cold.

Her voice was hesitant as she said, "We usually don't pray. It's just my dad and me. I don't usually sit down like this."

Andrew nodded understandingly and leaned forward to lift the lid off one of the serving dishes.

Jasmine touched his arm. "But I'd like it—if you could."

Andrew smiled at her. "Okay." But now it was his turn to be hesitant. "We, uh, usually hold hands to pray at home…" Andrew looked away, regretting the words the moment he'd spoken them. *How could I be so presumptuous?*

He felt her take his hand. "I'd like that," she said softly.

Andrew's heart surged with joy as he prayed, thanking the Lord for the meal and for their time together.

But it was over all too soon. And Andrew knew that he needed to get back to work.

"Maybe I could stop by tomorrow," he said.

Jasmine happily agreed. "Just don't suddenly appear like some monster looming out of the mists with a face mask on— and that helmet thing in your hand."

With a grin, Andrew held up two fingers for "scout's honor" as he quipped, "I promise not to come looming out of the mists." He reached for his coat. "I would like to fill up your woodstove in the morning for you, though."

"Oh, it's okay. I can manage."

"I'd *like* to do it."

Jasmine smiled. "Come in for coffee afterwards then."

He wanted to say something more. He didn't want their time together to be over. He wanted to kiss her goodbye or at least give her a hug.

He wanted to tell her that he loved her...

"I'll see you tomorrow," she said.

"Right, tomorrow. Okay then. I should go. I'll—uh—see you then."

Her kiss seemed to come from nowhere. It was probably meant for his cheek. It landed on his chin.

"Thanks for this evening—and this afternoon." She smiled up at him, seemingly unembarrassed that her kiss had missed its target. Maybe she'd meant to kiss him on the chin...

"Bye." Andrew quickly ducked out the door, more confused then ever.

As he turned and headed south on the Mine Road, Andrew thought that at least he would soon have plenty of time on his hands to think things through. He'd pretty much decided to stake out the Health Center that night. If the thief kept to the pattern he'd established, Andrew might be fortunate enough to catch him in the act.

And if not tonight, then maybe tomorrow or the next night. It was a bit of a long shot, but Andrew was quite sure that what was needed at this point was to actually see the crime in progress. There seemed to already be sufficient circumstantial evidence pointing to one person. What was needed now was cold hard proof—irrevocable, beyond a shadow of a doubt proof.

Colin was at the station when he stopped in there.

"How's it going?" he asked without looking directly at Andrew. It was the response Andrew had come to expect when anyone asked about the investigation. No one seemed to look him in the eye. He wondered how they would all feel when he made the arrest.

"If I have to make an arrest—" Andrew began.

"Call me. Any time of the day or night." His tone held no room for argument. Andrew, fresh from the academy, almost saluted and said, "Yes, sir!" Instead, he merely nodded.

Colin held his eye for a full moment before turning away. "You're getting close then?"

Andrew told him of his planned stakeout.

"Your mom could let you in," Colin suggested.

Andrew looked at his watch. "I should get started on that."

His uncle nodded, but seemed reluctant to let him go. "We're proud of you," he spoke gruffly. "And you still have that job if you want it—when all this is over."

"Yes, thank you." Andrew moved to go.

"You call me. Don't try anything on your own."

Andrew knew what he meant and didn't take offence. He nodded briefly, zipped up his jacket, and walked out into the cool night air.

As far back as he could remember, Andrew had admired his Uncle Colin and wanted to follow in his footsteps. It would be an honor to serve under his leadership.

And he would like to spend more time with Jasmine…

Andrew left his truck at home. His mother walked with him to the Health Center and unlocked the door for him. She handed him a thermos of coffee she'd made, smiled vaguely, patted him on the arm, and turned to go.

Andrew heard her relock the door from the outside. He had already chosen a place for the stakeout. A thorough search would reveal his hiding place, but Andrew was going on the assumption that the thief would want to get the drugs and get back out again as quickly as possible.

From where he was, Andrew could hear if anyone entered the Health Center. And the area would be clearly illuminated. There was always a light left on in the hallway and by the front entrance. The nurses' station was directly inside and the entrance light partially illuminated the area. Andrew was behind a file cabinet in the corner of the office. When the thief had his back turned removing items from the drug cupboard, Andrew would be able to sneak a glance out at him and see who it was. He would have to call for back-up before he made the arrest, so he would probably have to trail the suspect for a time after he left the building.

While he was waiting, Andrew had decided to catch up on some reading and had brought his pocket-sized Bible along. He'd been reading from the book of First Samuel and now continued on into Second Samuel, chapters that described the life of King David. What an extraordinary life he'd led from shepherd to giant-killer to king! He'd been called a man after God's own heart, but he had been anything but sinless. This had also been recorded for all to read for generations to come. And many unfair things had happened in David's life. Considered the runt of the litter by his father, criticized harshly by his older brothers, publicly mocked by his wife and betrayed by his own children, King David nevertheless still kept his heart seeking after God.

Andrew had read the book of Psalms through many times and knew this to be true. David, who was also an excellent musician, had poured out his soul as he wrote the songs, his honesty running through them all like a thread.

Andrew wondered if that was the key ingredient, or at least the starting off point, to the restoration of good healthy relationships—both with God and man. If people could just be honest with each other and with the Lord...

Andrew, determined now to finish Second Samuel, began to plow his way through the list of names in the second last chapter of the book. But he was having trouble staying focused. He'd drunk most of the coffee and had chanced a trip down the hall once to use the bathroom. Walking around had woken him up some, but he didn't want to risk being in the wrong place at the wrong time when the thief came—if he even did. Andrew had no way of knowing for sure. Andrew realized that he would have to get several hours of sleep the next day if he was planning to stay up another night.

He was getting very, very sleepy...

Suddenly, it was happening! Andrew felt a strange mix of both relief and dread. This was the moment he'd been waiting for—but was he really ready for it?

There was a loud *kerchunk* as the bolt drew back under the pressure from the key.

Andrew slipped the Bible into his pocket.

Then came the slight scrape of metal against metal as the main entrance door opened.

Andrew remained still and quiet as wet shoes made small squeaking sounds on the polished floor. Now onto the carpet... A slight pause, and then the rattle of keys again. Andrew could barely discern when the cabinet door was opened, but he could hear quite clearly the rattle of pills in containers being moved around.

Andrew glanced out.

His heart beat faster. He'd known. He'd known all along—hadn't he?

Or maybe just like the rest of the community, he'd only guessed.

Chapter 6

ANDREW DIDN'T MOVE UNTIL HE heard the door open and then close again. The key turned in the lock, driving the bolt back into place.

Andrew moved quickly now, dialing Colin's number on his cell phone as he hurried towards the door. He turned the bolt from the inside and stepped through.

Andrew had the cell phone to his ear. He heard a voice come on. "Hello…"

"In pursuit of suspect. Just outside the Health Center."

There was silence on the other end.

"Uncle Colin?"

A deep sigh. "Yeah, I'll be right there." Another long pause. "Does he have a vehicle—or is he walking?"

"He's on foot," Andrew answered. "He's heading towards the Mine Road. We're going to lose our light soon. I'll have to get closer."

"Okay, I'll meet you there."

"I'm on the Mine Road now."

But Colin had already clicked off his phone.

As the lights from the community faded, his uncle's words suddenly registered on Andrew. *I'll meet you there.* He knew where the suspect was going. He knew who the suspect was.

Colin's house was up ahead. The Peters' home was further along. If Colin had pulled out of his driveway before Doctor Peters walked past…

Andrew hurried a little to close the distance between the two of them.

There was no traffic at all on the road, at least from what Andrew could see or hear. If Uncle Colin was in his car, he must be quite some way ahead of them. Had he been sitting awake, fully clothed, waiting for Andrew's phone call? Andrew remembered his uncle saying something about being on night-shift…

Doctor Peters showed no sign that he knew he was being followed. Andrew had to actually walk a little slower than normal to keep apace with him.

Andrew could tell when Doctor Peters stepped onto the crushed rock of the driveway, but if there had been just a bit more snow, Andrew wouldn't have heard him at all.

Andrew was actually thankful for the snow. It would have been difficult to see the road without it—and virtually impossible to follow someone at this hour of the night. Or morning… Andrew glanced down at his watch—4:18 a.m.

From where he was, the house looked completely dark.

Jasmine must be asleep.

Andrew wondered if Colin would wake her to tell her that her father was being arrested. Colin… Where was he?

The wooden steps creaked slightly under the pressure of

Doctor Peters' feet. He was on the top step of three when a voice called.

"Is that you, Dad?" A light came on, the front door opened, and Jasmine appeared fully clothed.

Had no one slept this night?

A voice came out of the darkness. "Go back inside, Jasmine."

Colin…

Doctor Peters stood as if frozen in time.

Jasmine came out and stood beside him.

Her eyes darted between Colin on one side of the steps and Andrew on the other. "What's going on?" she demanded in a trembling voice.

"Jasmine, please go back inside," Colin said again.

Andrew walked up two steps to stand in front of Doctor Peters.

He knew where to look; he'd seen them being put there. Carefully, he removed the small bag of colored pills from the right lower pocket of Doctor Peters' winter coat. He took a step down, turned, and handed the bag to Colin.

Then taking a deep breath, Andrew turned back again and began: "Doctor Jeff Peters, you are under arrest for the theft and possession of—"

"No!" Jasmine launched herself at Andrew, throwing him off balance and knocking him into the snow. "You can't do this!" she yelled. "I trusted you."

Andrew struggled to his feet, but she hung on to him. Tears were pouring down her cheeks as she sobbed the words again, "I trusted you. I trusted you."

"Jasmine." Colin's voice was cold and official now. "You're

interfering with an arrest. Go back inside."

She stared wildly at him, then crumpled into tears, sinking down into the snow by Andrew's feet.

Andrew tore his eyes away from her and tried to bring his runaway emotions back under control. He was a trained RCMP officer. He had a job to do. But he was breathing hard and when he spoke, the words came out in short bursts. "Dr. Peters—you are—under arrest—for—"

"It's okay," Colin interrupted him in a tired voice. "I'll take it from here."

Colin spoke into a handset. "Keegan? Yeah, we've made the arrest. Bring a cruiser 'round. Yeah, Jeff Peters' house."

Andrew felt as if he'd had the wind punched out of him. "He knew," Andrew gasped. "*You* knew! *Everyone* knew! What'd you need me for—a fall guy?"

Colin looked away. "We didn't know for sure," he muttered.

Doctor Peters had remained where he was, seemingly untouched by the storm of emotions swirling around him. Jasmine was still on her knees in the snow—with no coat on. It was a cold night.

Andrew took off his uniform coat and put it around her shoulders.

Jasmine shrugged it off as she staggered to her feet. "Leave me alone!" she yelled. "Just leave me alone!" She walked up the steps to stand beside her father and looked down at Colin imploringly. "You can't arrest him…"

"Jasmine," Colin said in a gentle but firm voice, "your father needs help. We've tried—all of us. This will force the issue. He'll have to go into treatment."

Tears were still streaming down her cheeks as she leaned with her back against the door of her house.

"It's okay," her father said, speaking for the first time, his voice sad and low.

Jasmine stared at him for a moment. Then she ran into the house, slamming the door behind her.

Andrew moved to follow her, but Colin's tired voice intercepted him. "We'll call her sister. She'll come over."

A cruiser pulled into the driveway. "I'll call her," Andrew said as he bent to pick up his discarded RCMP uniform coat.

It was Joshua's sleepy voice that answered on the fifth ring. But he was instantly awake when Andrew explained the situation. "We'll be right over."

Doctor Peters was escorted into the police vehicle. No cuffs were used. There was no protest of any kind from the older man.

As the car's headlights faded, Andrew turned towards the house.

How had he let this happen? How had he let himself be suckered into this situation? He'd been set up, big time! His uncle knew what was going to happen. Had he not known—or had he just not cared—that Andrew and Jasmine were falling in love?

Joshua and Missy arrived together. "Where are they?" Missy asked breathlessly.

"Your father is at the station," Andrew said, trying hard to swallow back his own emotions. "Jasmine…" He could barely say her name. "She's inside."

Missy looked around. "Alone? Why aren't you in there with her?"

"I—" Andrew felt sick to his stomach. "I arrested her— your—father."

But Missy was already walking up the steps. She went inside, shutting the door behind her.

Andrew sank down onto the bottom step. Joshua sat down beside him.

For a moment neither spoke. Then Joshua ventured, "Kind of rough for you."

The understatement of the year!

There was silence again. Snowflakes began to drift downwards.

Joshua said, "We can stay now. If you need to go—do reports…"

Andrew didn't know how he could ever stomach going back to the station—facing his uncle—facing the rest of the police force—facing the community.

He stood slowly to his feet, put his coat back on, and began the long walk back.

"Hey!" Joshua called.

Andrew looked back.

"You want a ride?"

Andrew shook his head.

He was glad for the walk. He needed to be alone—to think.

It had been a mistake to come back. He would find a job somewhere else—where no one knew him—and where he didn't know anyone else.

He could be a good police officer. Andrew knew that in his heart. But not in his home community—not amongst his family—and friends.

He almost turned in at his parent's house. He wondered if they really needed him at the police station. Most of the report was done and sent in already—just the stakeout and arrest needed to be documented. Andrew wondered if he would even be listed as the arresting officer. In the end, it had been Colin and Keegan who had helped Doctor Peters into the cruiser.

It was finally only Andrew's keen sense of duty that took his feet all the way to the police station.

His uncle was waiting for him. He looked exhausted. But Andrew could find no pity in his heart for him.

He slumped down into the chair at the desk that had been assigned to him, turned on the computer, and unlocked the drawer, taking out the hard copy of his file.

"It wasn't supposed to be you."

Andrew slammed the desk drawer shut.

"We thought they would send someone else—from outside the community."

Andrew stared at the screen.

"He's done so much for so many people. Your sister and Michael and so many others—they would have just died—"

Andrew turned to face him. "I know all that! I've known Doctor Peters—and his family—all of my life. I know what he's done for this community!"

Colin nodded slowly. "I didn't realize—about Jasmine—and you."

Andrew hit each computer key as if his finger was a hammer. Open—folder—open—file. Now his fingers hit like raindrops on a tin roof. Date—time—location—procedure.

"If you need me for anything…"

Andrew ignored him.

Colin's voice was barely audible. "…I'll be at home."

In the stillness of the now silent police station, Andrew could feel his heart beating like a steel drum. In this building, locked up in a cell, was Jasmine's father.

There was one guard on duty—an older fellow Andrew recognized as Constable Quequish. He carefully avoided Andrew's eye, fixing his attention on the far wall as he sat back in his chair, a cup of coffee in his hand.

Andrew wrote a thorough report, going over what he'd written before as well. He wasn't the least bit tired anymore and he wanted to get it done and over with once and for all.

By the time Constable Quequish set a cup of coffee on the desk beside him, Andrew was cooled off enough to acknowledge his kind gesture with a word of thanks.

The new shift was coming on when Andrew finally finished everything to his satisfaction. He e-mailed in his report and his supervisor called him a moment later.

"Get some rest," she advised, "and then we'll make arrangements for transporting the prisoner."

Andrew groaned inwardly. If he had to escort Doctor Peters to the airport and off the Reserve in handcuffs…

"Get some rest," his supervisor repeated. "You've had a long night. Call me later this afternoon. We need some time to make arrangements on our end anyway."

Andrew ended the call. He put all the information in a large envelope, sealed it, and locked it into the desk drawer, then handed the keys over to Constable Quequish.

But he might as well have left the drawer unlocked. Everyone in the community would know before noon that Doctor Peters was arrested—and would know what the charges were—if they didn't know already.

His mother and father were sitting at the kitchen table when Andrew walked in. By the looks on their faces, *they* already knew.

His mother stood up. "Is there anything I can get you?"

Andrew shook his head, walked into his room, and shut the door. He flopped down on the lower bunk bed and closed his eyes.

But it was several hours before sleep finally overtook him.

IT SEEMED AS IF NO TIME had passed at all.

His parents were sitting at the table once again.

But there was the smell of supper in the air and the dim light outside was that of twilight and not of dawn.

She'd made his favorite meal—pot roast. It was from a moose that his dad had shot in the fall. She was serving some up for him now, talking all the while. "We already ate. We thought it best to just let you sleep … "

Andrew looked at his watch, groaned, and began to put his coat on. He needed to get down to the station. He'd told his supervisor that he'd call. At least he still had his uniform on.

"Wait, Andrew!" His mother called as he reached for the doorknob. "If you're planning to go to the station … Colin left a message for you. He talked with the RCMP. The—uh—arrangements have already been made … " Her voice trailed off to a whisper.

Andrew's father stood up and put his arm around her. "The

plane left about an hour ago," he said.

Andrew took off his coat and boots and sat down at the table.

He started to eat, but the food just seemed to stick in his throat.

He looked over at his parents. "What's going to happen to him, do you think?"

Neither spoke for a moment. Then his father began, "The judge may go easy on him. It's a first offence and there are extenuating circumstances."

"And there'll be no shortage of character references," his mother added.

"Normally," his father said slowly, "it would mean a lengthy prison term."

"But in Jeff—Doctor Peters'—case," his mother continued, "the judge could possibly decide that a treatment program would be sufficient. And he will likely be restricted from working at the Health Center."

"He was still working there?" Andrew asked incredulously. From what he'd seen of Doctor Peters, he would have thought that was impossible.

"Jeff was—is—one of the best neonatal surgeons in the world," his mother said.

"He was called in occasionally," his father added.

"For special cases."

Andrew had to smile. He'd forgotten how his mom and dad had the habit of finishing each other's sentences. If you were sitting between them, you could get dizzy looking back and forth as they spoke.

He'd always thought he would get married someday—when

the right girl came along…

"Andrew…" His mother's voice was gentle.

He looked up at her.

"We know this has been hard for you."

Andrew shook his head. He didn't want their compassion. They were part of the problem. They knew about the thefts. They knew about Jasmine and her father's problems. Everyone had insulated or ignored them. No one had helped them to face the issues in their lives. No one had cared enough to find out what was wrong with Jasmine and to help her through it. No one had confronted her father and forced him to seek help.

"I'm probably going to head out tomorrow—maybe look for a job in Kenora or Winnipeg."

Both of his parents protested at the same time.

Andrew gave them a sardonic grin. "I think I've done enough damage here, don't you think?"

"You did the right thing, son," his father said earnestly. "People in the community will respect that."

Andrew shook his head. "I arrested her father!"

"Maybe it will help her, too," his mother said. "Jasmine's been holed up in that cabin all winter. She doesn't even clean her house or do laundry. All she does is eat—"

Andrew stood up quick enough for his chair to go flying backwards.

"You never really liked her, did you?"

"No, that's not true," his mother protested.

The phone ringing at that instant prevented a further exchange of words.

Bill answered it and a moment later handed the phone to

Andrew. "It's for you, son."

"Andrew?" Missy's anxious voice came through the receiver. "Have you heard from Jasmine?"

"Why would I hear from her?" Andrew asked angrily.

"I thought—I thought maybe she would call or you would go over. You guys have been spending some time together—and you've always been friends—"

Andrew could hardly believe what he was hearing. "That was before last night!" he almost shouted. "You were there. You saw what happened! Why are you even calling me?"

"I haven't heard from her—not since this morning," Missy continued fretfully. "She doesn't answer her phone and she has the door locked. I have a key—but do you think I should just barge in? She might have finally fallen asleep. You know she doesn't sleep very well—"

No, he didn't. But it would explain why she looked so tired all the time.

"I'm worried about her," Missy continued. "But I don't really know what to do. Joshua thought that maybe I should call you."

Andrew sank down into the easy chair. His eyes focused on the woodstove.

Had anyone thought to put wood into the Peters' woodstove?

"When did you last see her?" Andrew asked.

Missy hesitated before answering. "Jasmine asked us to leave almost right away—after the arrest. She said that she wanted to be alone—"

Andrew jumped to his feet. "So you just left her?"

"She insisted."

But Andrew didn't want to hear any more. "I gotta go," he muttered.

"Will you go see her? Do you want the key?"

"I don't know. I'll talk to you later." He hung up the phone. It *didn't* seem right to unlock her door if she refused to open it. He, for sure, couldn't do it. It might be okay if her sister did… But what he could, and would, do was check to make sure that Jasmine at least had some heat in her house.

Chapter 7

BEFORE LEAVING THE HOUSE, Andrew changed out of his uniform. On the off chance that Jasmine would see him, he wanted to make it clear he was there as her friend, not as an RCMP officer.

Pulling into her driveway, Andrew noted with dismay that there was no smoke at all coming from the outdoor woodstove; the fire was completely out.

For how long? And how cold must it be inside the house by now?

Quickly Andrew made his way towards the woodstove. If he had to start with wet wood, it might be difficult...

He opened the firebox. It was completely dead—not an ember remained.

Andrew looked around and finally found what he needed. Off to the side of the woodpile, partially buried in snow, was a small container of used oil. He found an old newspaper in Colin's truck and, shaking the snow off some of the smaller pieces of wood, Andrew began to carefully set the fire. He stacked the wood so that air could pass over the oil soaked paper and around and through the pieces of wood.

Andrew made sure the fire was burning well before closing the door of the firebox and heading back towards the house.

He knocked tentatively at first, then more loudly when he received no answer. He tried calling her on his cell phone as well and left a message on her answering machine. If she was in the room and could hear it…

Andrew waited a bit longer, trying to think of what he should do.

He went back and checked the fire. It was going well.

He came around the front and knocked again. He tried the door. It was locked. He called her on the phone again—and left another message. And waited a while longer.

Finally, Andrew decided to go. He'd left her his cell phone number. She could call him. He had to allow her some right to privacy—to be alone if she wanted.

As he pulled out of the drive, Andrew found himself heading north instead of south. Joshua had always been a good friend. And Andrew felt he should talk to Missy—tell her that he had at least tried to get hold of Jasmine.

They must have heard him drive up. Missy opened the door even before he knocked. She seemed very relieved to see him and invited him in right away.

Andrew didn't feel like making it into a social occasion. If they had invited him to sit at the kitchen table or over by the fireplace, Andrew knew he would probably have refused, but when Joshua sat down at one of the dining room tables close by the door and motioned him over, Andrew reluctantly joined him.

He kept his coat on, though. Missy read his mood quite well.

"You're angry with us," she said.

Andrew avoided the question. "The fire was out. I started it again."

"Thanks for doing that," Joshua said. "I should have thought of it."

"Did you see her?" Missy asked anxiously.

Andrew shook his head. He told them that he'd knocked on her door and that it was still locked.

Missy stood up quickly and walked across the room. She came back a moment later with a key in her hand. She laid it on the table beside Andrew. "I have another one," she said.

"I wouldn't feel right…"

Missy leaned towards him. "Jasmine connected with you—in a way that she has never connected with either of us. At least not since—" Her voice broke.

Joshua put his hand gently on top of hers. He looked over at Andrew. "Did Jasmine tell you about… the sexual assault?"

Andrew nodded.

Missy blinked back tears. "You probably think that we don't care—that we haven't tried to help her."

"Have you?"

"Yes, of course we have!" Missy almost shouted. "And we've had quite a few other things we've had to deal with as well. It hasn't been easy."

"Yes, this empire you're building here."

"It's not an empire," Joshua spoke quietly.

Andrew immediately regretted his words. He knew the work that Missy and Joshua were doing couldn't be done except with a heart of love.

"But it seems wrong to neglect your family," he still couldn't help saying.

"We haven't neglected our family—none of them," Joshua said. "One of my nieces was in the program this past winter. And I have two other young nieces. Their mother is no longer living and their father is in prison. Your Uncle Colin and Aunt Sarah have adopted them. But I still consider them partly my responsibility and we try to visit them often."

Andrew shook his head impatiently. "I know all that. Just tell me what you've done—if anything—to help Jasmine."

"Andrew," Missy interjected, "We *have* tried to help Jasmine. But what you need to see and understand is the broader picture. It's not all our fault. Your sister got married to my cousin and neither Missy nor our dad came to the wedding. I can't imagine how Uncle David and Aunt Cora felt."

Andrew jumped to his feet, angrier than he'd been in a long time. "So you're punishing her for not coming to the wedding?"

Joshua's voice sounded old and tired. And strangely like the former owner of the lodge, Grandpa Tom. "Sit down, Andrew."

Andrew sat.

Joshua turned towards Missy. "Honey, could you make us all some coffee? And maybe we could have some of that delicious apple pie you made yesterday?"

Andrew could almost feel a lecture from his grandpa coming...

But when he spoke, Joshua suddenly sounded young again—young, inexperienced, and a little overwhelmed by it all. And he was appealing to Andrew as a friend. "This time last year, I was where you are. I really only had myself to be responsible for. Tom had the weight of the load here at the camp and even though we shared the same vision, I always felt that he would be the one ultimately responsible. And if not him, then his son, Jeff."

Andrew listened, interested in spite of himself.

Joshua shook his head. "I was in no way prepared for the responsibility that was suddenly thrust upon me last summer. Even in my own family, dysfunctional as it was, Russell was the one everyone looked up to—and feared. Now it's not just my family, but Missy's family as well that I feel responsible for. And you may or may not see the importance of the ministry we had here this past winter for local youth—"

Andrew looked around. "It's not going on now?"

"We're taking a break for now," Joshua said. "There's a lot of work and planning that has to go into something like this—and in some ways, it was a trial period for us." Joshua smiled. "We need time to recoup and see what we want to do differently. We also want to do some staff training. There's a seven-step program…"

Andrew stood up again. "Joshua, I can appreciate what you're saying. But right now, my only concern is for Jasmine."

"She could benefit from this."

Andrew looked down at him doubtfully.

"It's a structured support group that meets once a week for two hours. Rosalee and Michael, and Missy and I, ran through it all in one three-day period, but it's best if it's stretched over seven weeks. It leaves time for the healing process to take place in each person's life."

Missy set coffee, cream and sugar, and three pieces of pie down on the table as Joshua continued. "I think that it helped

Missy and me a lot—as a couple."

Missy nodded her agreement. "It really made me understand Joshua better. He'd told me some of what he'd gone through, but not all—and I really had no concept of how it had affected him— how it affected even our marriage."

"You guys have a good marriage," Andrew protested as he pulled out a chair and sat down again.

Joshua raised an eyebrow. "And you've been here how many days?"

"Well, I saw you at the wedding… And besides, no one's mentioned—"

"Yeah right, the old moccasin telegraph." Joshua grinned. "Well, we do have a good marriage." Joshua reached for Missy's hand and they exchanged affectionate looks before he turned back to speak to Andrew again. "But a good marriage can always be made better. And there're some things I know I still need to deal with from my past. And," he conceded, "there are also things in our marriage that we still both need to work through together."

Andrew took a sip of his coffee. "So you think this program might help Jasmine deal with what happened to her?"

"Yes," they both answered at the same time.

Andrew smiled. The only possible thing worse than finishing each other's sentences was when a married couple said the same thing at the same time!

"Great minds think alike!" Andrew quipped as he took a bite of pie.

"Fools seldom differ," Joshua returned.

"Hey, speak for yourself!" Missy punched him playfully on the shoulder.

"Umm, great pie," Joshua said with a grin as he lifted his fork to his mouth.

They ate the rest of their pie in companionable silence. Then Joshua stood to his feet. "I'll get you a copy of the seven-step program," he said.

He didn't have far to go. It was on the desk that Grandma Peters had always used.

"This place doesn't seem the same without them," Andrew spoke sadly.

Missy didn't need to ask who "them" was. Her grandfather had built the camp and he and his wife and youngest son had lived there for over twenty years.

"How is Grandma Peters? And Bobby?" Andrew added, referring to the older couple's mentally challenged son.

Missy smiled. "They're doing good. They live in an apartment that's on the ground floor of Uncle David and Aunt Cora's house. Actually, I think Aunt Cora really appreciates having a live-in babysitter for Alisha."

Andrew looked around again. "It just seems so quiet."

"Well, that certainly isn't how it usually is around here!" Missy declared. "As Joshua said, we're on a bit of a break right now. But we're planning some staff training. Part of that will be this seven-week support group. When our next batch of youth arrive, our staff will divide into pairs and form three support groups specifically focusing on the issues these youth are facing."

Andrew flipped through the binder of material. "And this is what you're thinking of for Jasmine?" he asked.

"Yes," Joshua replied. "It may be the one thing that could help her face up to the problems in her life."

Andrew rubbed his forehead. "She always says that she can manage."

"Yes, I've heard that a lot," Missy agreed.

"We'll be having our first meeting this Wednesday at seven o'clock," Joshua said, resting his hand on the binder.

"Could you maybe speak to Jasmine about it—see what she thinks?" Missy asked tentatively.

"As if she'll ever speak to me again—after what I did last night!"

"He's my dad, too," Missy spoke softly. "And I'm speaking to you."

"It's five days away," Joshua added.

"Hey," Missy said with a grin, "we Peters women are pretty stubborn, but we do come around eventually."

"Yeah, look, she married me!" Joshua declared.

"Uh-huh, as I recall you were the one that needed convincing…"

Andrew stood to go. Normally he would enjoy their friendly banter. But all he could think about now was Jasmine—all alone in that house—her father arrested—by him.

Andrew heard the scrape of their chairs as they stood up. He turned to say goodbye.

Their faces sober again, Missy and Joshua thanked him for stopping by. Missy pressed the key into his hands and Joshua encouraged him once again to talk to Jasmine about the seven-week support group.

When Andrew left, he wasn't sure where he was going.

He drove up and down the road, finally turning into Jasmine's driveway, telling himself that he should check on the woodstove at least once more tonight.

The fire was roaring—as he'd expected.

Andrew walked around to the front of the house. There were still no lights on, though it was getting dark. He knocked on the door, waited, and knocked again. He fingered the key in his pocket. What if Jasmine was hurt?

Just as he was about to put the key into the lock, he saw a light go on in the back of the house. Relieved, Andrew pocketed the key once more and walked back to his truck.

He still wasn't sure what he wanted to do or where he wanted to go.

Indecision led to inaction. Andrew was warm enough in his big parka, sheltered from the wind and snow in the cab of the truck.

He thought about Jasmine and what her sister and brother-in-law had said. Andrew still doubted if she'd ever speak to him again, but maybe Missy was right. Maybe Jasmine just needed time.

But if Andrew was the one person that she had finally opened up to after all this time—and he had betrayed her—how could she ever again trust him or anyone else? Maybe it would be kinder to her if he just left the community. Missy and Joshua might eventually convince her to get the help she needed.

Andrew decided to check on the fire one more time and then head out. He'd give Missy her key back. There wasn't anything more he could do.

Andrew added another log to the fire, stuffing it in around the red, glowing logs already filling the firebox.

He had buckled on his seatbelt and was about to start the

engine when he heard a familiar beep. He'd missed a call!

Angry with himself for leaving his cell phone behind, Andrew quickly accessed his messages. His heart lurched as he heard Jasmine's weak, hesitant voice.

"Andrew—it's me. I can't go on anymore. I tried but—but I just—can't…"

Jasmine! With trembling fingers, Andrew unlocked his seatbelt and wrenched the car door open, the cell phone still pressed to his ear.

"I don't even know why I'm calling. Maybe I just wanted to say—goodbye."

Chapter 8

HE WAS AT THE DOOR IN AN INSTANT, the key in his hand.

Andrew thought he heard a faint cry even as he turned the key in the lock.

As he swung open the door, there was a groan and another low cry.

Then he saw her…

Jasmine was half-laying, half-sitting on the kitchen floor pressed up against a corner cupboard. A circle of blood was growing wider as it soaked through the white t-shirt she was wearing.

Andrew lunged forward to grab the knife from her hand.

HE WAS FIGHTING WITH HER. It wasn't fair! She shouldn't have called him!

He was pulling it away!

Ignoring the pain that threatened to consume her, Jasmine summoned all her strength and thrust down hard with the knife. It met resistance and Jasmine knew she had finally succeeded.

Strangely, she had needed his help to plunge the knife deep into her own body. She could feel the warm blood flowing beneath her hand.

Jasmine closed her eyes. She could let herself go now. The pain would be over soon. It would all be over.

Her body felt weighted. She was unable to move. Was this death?

She heard a low groan and opened her eyes. Andrew...

Andrew! He was on top of her—unconscious—or dead.

The warm blood still flowing—*it was Andrew's!*

The knife was in the upper part of his leg. Ignoring her own pain, Jasmine lifted his inert body away enough for her to press down hard around the wound.

"Andrew!" she sobbed. "Andrew..."

Her vision was blurred with tears, but she kept her hands steady and the pressure constant. Soon, the blood that had been literally pumping out of him was wet and sticky. The flow of fresh warm blood had been abated.

Andrew's face was as pale as death. And he wasn't moving at all.

Jasmine tried to determine if his chest was rising and falling. But he had on a big parka. He was so pale...

She had to get help!

Frantically, Jasmine looked around for the phone. It had been beside her on the floor. She'd called Andrew...

There it was! Jasmine switched hands, pressing down hard on the wound with her left hand and reaching out for the phone with her right. It had been pushed away during their struggle and was just barely in reach now. She pulled it closer with her fingertips and then picked it up in her hand.

But she was moving too slowly or the world around her was slowing and she was moving... Jasmine tried to think clearly... But her thoughts kept tumbling over each other.

Keep pressure on the wound. Call Sarah. Sarah's a nurse. Call Sarah...

"Hello."

"Sarah... Help..."

"Jasmine? Jasmine—what's wrong?"

"I killed him... I didn't mean to..."

"Killed who? Jasmine—is somebody there with you?"

"It shouldn't have been him... It shouldn't have been Andrew..."

"*Andrew!* Jasmine, tell me where you are! Are you at your house? Honey, you've *got* to tell me where you are."

Where you are... Where you are... Tile floor... Cupboard... Kitchen... House...

"House... My house..."

"Your house? Okay, Jasmine, Colin is using his radiophone. Help is on its way. Can you still hear me, Jasmine?"

"I'm pressing—down..."

"Pressing down?—Applying pressure! Is that what you're doing, Jasmine? Are you applying pressure to a wound? Colin, keep talking to her—I've got to get over there. *Pray for us!*"

"Jasmine, this is Colin. Sarah's on her way. You're going to be okay..."

"Andrew..."

"Andrew's going to be okay, too. People are on their way to help you. I called the station on my cell phone while you were talking to Sarah. Keegan is on his way right now. And they'll call your sister. And the Health Center. Doctor Morgan's in this week. He'll help you—and Andrew. Just hang in there…"

Pressure—she had to keep pressure—on the wound…

Jasmine dropped the phone. The voice kept talking—further away now…

She had to keep the pressure on—keep—pressure—on…

"I'M HER SISTER. I should have stayed with her. Or used my key…"

Joshua kept both hands on the steering wheel as he careened around the corner onto the gravel driveway. "We didn't know," he said. "We still don't know anything really. Just that Jasmine or Andrew is hurt…"

Andrew's truck was in the driveway, the driver's door wide open. The house door was open, too.

Joshua jumped onto the top step, ran around the corner into the kitchen, and stopped dead…

It was happening all over again.

The woman's eyes met his. Then she fell into the pool of blood, the knife still in her hand.

No. That's not the way it was.

The knife had been in his hand, not hers….

"Joshua…?"

It wasn't them. It wasn't his parents.

He wasn't four years old…
Missy needed his help.

Joshua forced himself to move forward and cleared his mind enough to help Missy lift Jasmine up so they could have a clearer view of her injuries—and Andrew's.

Sarah rushed in at that moment and Joshua gratefully let her take charge. She had a first aid kit with her and, working quickly, donned gloves before applying a sterile pressure bandage to Andrew's upper leg.

Jasmine was mumbling incoherently. Missy remained kneeling beside her, speaking words of reassurance.

"Get on the phone," Sarah ordered. "Call the Health Center."

There was blood on the phone, but Joshua didn't hesitate even a moment.

"Ask to speak directly to Doctor Morgan—if he's still there. He might be on his way already."

Joshua was through to the Health Center even before Sarah finished speaking. A moment later, Doctor Morgan was on the line.

"Got him," Joshua said.

"Tell him it's a knife wound to the femoral artery and the patient is unconscious."

Joshua quickly repeated her words into the phone.

"Blood type?" Joshua asked, relaying Doctor Morgan's question.

"They can call his mom. It should be on file as well. He was born there…"

Joshua was repeating her words as fast as she could speak

them, anticipating the answers she gave. His mom would for sure know his blood type—but she might be on her way over already. Colin would likely already have called his sister.

Police sirens blared, coming closer. A moment later, Keegan Littledeer and Damian Meekis rushed in.

"Got things under control?" Keegan asked Sarah.

"As much as can be," she said grimly. "He's lost a lot of blood."

"The doctor's on his way," Joshua added.

"What about her?" Keegan motioned towards Jasmine.

Missy was kneeling by his sister. "She's conscious but seems confused. I can't make out what she's saying. There's a lot of blood, but I think it's mostly Andrew's. Jasmine, can you hear me?"

Joshua was still feeling shaken by the vivid flashback he'd experienced. It had helped to be busy doing something. Now he stepped back a little as the door sprang open and Doctor Morgan burst in.

The older man started an IV on Andrew and listened as Sarah gave him an update on Andrew's condition. "Get Kenora on the phone," he ordered Keegan. "We'll need an air ambulance STAT."

Keegan began speaking into his radiophone as yet more people arrived on the scene. Jamie and Bill, Andrew's parents, moved into what was becoming a very crowded area. Joshua backed away further into the adjoining living room.

Jamie sounded close to hysteria. "She's killed him. She's killed my son!"

Jasmine raised her head. "No, it was an accident!" She sank

weakly back onto the floor. "I didn't mean to," she whispered faintly.

Jamie's voice carried over Missy's softly spoken assurances to her sister.

"How do you *accidentally* knife someone?" Jamie almost screamed the words.

Her husband Bill and Officer Meekis moved to either side of her, speaking in calm voices while Sarah tried to reassure her that Andrew was still alive.

The doctor's reaction was more severe. "Get her out of here," he ordered.

"No," Jamie spoke in a voice that only trembled slightly, "I'll be quiet."

Sarah remained working over Andrew, but the doctor turned his attention to Jasmine.

"Why isn't he helping Andrew?" Jamie's frantic whisper reached across the room. "He's the one that got knifed—all because he arrested her father!"

The doctor threw Jamie an angry look but continued to examine Jasmine. "How old are you?" he asked her.

"I didn't mean to do it!" Jasmine whimpered.

"She's eighteen," Missy spoke up.

The doctor's voice was surprisingly gentle. "It would be better if she would answer the questions." He turned back to Jasmine, moving his hands over her abdomen as he spoke. "Is this your first?"

There was a sudden hush in the room. All eyes were riveted on Jasmine. Her frightened nod unleashed a storm of protest.

"She's not pregnant!"

"She couldn't be!"

"I'm her sister—I would know."

"Everyone would know…"

The doctor raised his hand, signaling for silence. Then he spoke to Keegan. "Notify dispatch that we require transportation for two patients. Can I talk to them on that phone of yours?"

"Even if she is pregnant, she doesn't need help. My son—"

"Get her out of here now!" the doctor yelled.

Sarah looked up. "Jamie, you'll probably be able to go on the helicopter with Andrew. Maybe you could go home and get some things together."

Bill smiled gratefully at Sarah. "Yes, and we need to get hold of Katie at her friend's house. And Rosalee and Michael…" The sound of his voice faded as they moved towards the door.

Doctor Morgan spoke into Keegan's radiophone. "We have two patients. A nineteen-year-old male with incision to right femoral artery. No popliteal pulse detected. Carotid pulse rapid and thready. Patient remains unconscious. Also an eighteen-year-old primigravida with possible perforation of the uterine wall. Please alert obstetrics for possible premature delivery of twins."

"No! No! No!" Jasmine's cries turned into low moans. Missy bent over her and Joshua rushed to her side as well.

"That was a mistake," the doctor said more to himself than anyone else. Joshua looked up, meeting the older man's eyes as he continued, "She didn't know?"

"She must have known about the pregnancy. But twins…" Joshua's voice trailed off. It still seemed impossible that she had kept it secret. Everyone had just thought that she was gaining a lot of weight. She'd even kept it from her sister. But the twins must be a surprise even to Jasmine…

Missy was smoothing back her hair, talking softly to her, doing her best to calm her down, but Jasmine continued to sob uncontrollably.

Keegan had the radiophone again. "There's a helicopter in the area," he announced. "They can be here in five minutes. They want to know where the nearest spot is to land."

"So soon!" Joshua exclaimed.

"They had a false alarm. Some kid was choking. They got there and the kid was running around playing." Keegan spoke into the radiophone again, "Probably the airport is your best bet—"

"No, wait," Joshua said, "it'd be closer for them to land by the lodge."

Keegan offered Joshua the phone and he gave the pilot directions. "There's an old mine headframe, and a little north of that is the lodge. Between the two, you'll see an open field. There's only a couple of inches of snow on it."

Joshua handed the phone to Keegan and turned his attention back to Jasmine. Her crying had subsided, replaced by low moans. "I can't… I can't…"

"We're going to help you through this," Joshua tried to reassure her.

But it was as if she hadn't heard.

Keegan bent down beside them. His voice was low. "I need to write up a report." He glanced over at the doctor. "Can she answer any questions?"

Doctor Morgan shook his head. "Not a good idea."

But Jasmine wanted to speak. "I didn't mean to do it!"

"Jasmine, I have to write down what you're saying," Keegan said gently. "You're not under arrest, but you could be at some point. Do you understand?"

Missy protested, loudly defending her sister, but Joshua put a hand on her arm. "Honey, it might be best if Jasmine tells it her way."

"I wasn't trying to hurt Andrew," Jasmine said in a fragile voice, her eyes still focused on Keegan. "I wanted to—to end my pregnancy. I thought I could go through with it—arrange an adoption or something. But in the end, I couldn't bear it. I tried to kill it—them... Andrew came in. We fought with the knife and..." Jasmine's eyes filled with tears once more and her voice trailed off to a whisper. "He wasn't the one who was supposed to die."

Joshua turned away, suddenly overcome with grief. It had been that way with his parents. They had fought. His drunken father had been hurting Joshua's baby sister. His mother, also intoxicated, had grabbed a knife to attack his father. But in the ensuing battle, she had been the one who had died. The courts had ruled manslaughter...

People were moving around. The paramedics had arrived.

Missy wanted to go with her sister. Andrew's mother was back, wanting to go with her son.

Chapter 9

JAMIE HAD GONE ON THE HELICOPTER with Andrew. Bill and Kaitlyn would fly down later. Missy went along with Jasmine to the Health Center while Joshua stayed to talk with Keegan for a while.

Though he and Missy had been the first ones to arrive on the scene, Joshua knew there wasn't much more information that he could provide for Keegan. Jasmine's statement had given them a fairly clear picture of what had happened. It had been an accident, but if Andrew died, there could be an arrest. And it would be up to the judge to decide if Jasmine's story was the truth. And even then, she could be charged with manslaughter.

Joshua looked around the kitchen. It looked like something out of a low budget horror film. He would have to see about someone helping him clean it up. He wondered when the police would allow him to do this. It was, he supposed, a crime scene. But maybe if no one died—and if no one pressed charges…

Joshua's mind was filled with "if onlys." If only he had stopped by earlier. If only they had insisted that Jasmine get some help. If only they had done *something* different than they had!

It was impossible not to voice what was in his heart.

Keegan understood. "There's so many times, as a police officer, you think back and wonder if maybe you should have gone a little bit harder on a first time offender... Sometimes when you finally make the arrest, it's already too late. Somebody's been hurt bad.

"I know you and Missy tried to help Jasmine," Keegan continued. "Maybe now, you feel like it wasn't enough. But this past winter, you were helping other people—like my brother and his wife. Sometimes it's just not possible to help everyone."

Joshua knew in his mind that what Keegan was saying was true. But still his heart rebelled. Right now, it didn't seem much consolation that he'd helped others when his own sister-in-law had been driven to the point of suicide and he hadn't even seen it coming.

JASMINE FELT LIKE A LUMP OF CARGO being transferred from place to place. They were just doing their job. She knew that. But everyone seemed to know what had happened and didn't know quite how to treat her. They spoke in hushed voices *about* her, but not directly *to* her.

And now that she had arrived at the hospital, Jasmine wished desperately to know how Andrew was doing, but felt that she had no right to ask.

She couldn't go anywhere on her own. They had her attached to a bunch of stuff—an IV and some monitors. One was a fetal heart monitor attached to a belt around her waist. They'd had a hard time finding a spot to place the monitor because of the large bandage covering the knife wounds.

They'd put some local anesthetic around the area before stitching her up and they'd given her some pain medication through the IV as well.

Jasmine was still feeling the effects of the pain medication. It made her a little drowsy and disoriented, but it had little effect on the regular waves of pain that seemed to arise suddenly out of nowhere, threatening to consume her. It was happening again and Jasmine braced herself for its onslaught, forcing back the groan that was in her throat.

She didn't want to wake Missy, who was dozing in a chair beside her bed. She'd already thrown up once this morning. Two nights in a row, she'd been woken in the night to a family emergency. Jasmine had already decided that when Joshua arrived, she would ask him to take Missy home. They, unlike her, did want to keep their baby.

But it wasn't just a baby with Jasmine—it was *babies*. As if God didn't think it cruel enough for her to have become pregnant, He had to twist the knife and make it not just one but two of them!

Jasmine tried to twist away from the pain that was consuming her body and soul. The monitors attached to her belly began to beep and Jasmine quickly tried to realign herself again, but it was too late. Whatever she'd done was done and a nurse was coming in to examine her.

"You need to lie still," the nurse said with a slight edge in her voice as she adjusted the monitor.

Jasmine nodded, wishing the woman would just leave. The physical pain had receded again, but the hollow ache inside her remained.

Missy was awake now, too. She didn't look much better than she had before her nap. "Is there some place you could lie down?" Jasmine asked her.

"No, I'm fine," Missy replied.

The nurse spoke kindly to her. "We have a visitor's room down the hall. You would be welcome to use that. They tell me you're expecting a baby as well. Your first?" Missy was ushered out into the hallway.

Jasmine felt nothing but relief.

She lay still, careful not to set off the alarms again.

She wanted to be alone.

She should have stayed alone tonight. Whatever had possessed her to call Andrew? She should have known he would come running—try to stop her. It wasn't what she had wanted.

But nothing had gone the way she had wanted.

She hadn't wanted to be raped and she certainly hadn't wanted to become pregnant when she was just seventeen years old.

She'd thought often about ending the pregnancy, but hadn't been able to bring herself to actually do it.

All her life, she had heard about Rachel's Children—an organization her family was involved with that rescued children from abortion. Jasmine's father had worked for Rachel's Children and her sister Missy had been one of the rescued babies. For Jasmine to abort her child—children—would have seemed like a betrayal against her own family and all that they had worked for and believed in.

Jasmine could possibly have done it if the nurse had offered her the "morning after" pill in the emergency room right after the rape. But somehow in the confusion, with the search for next-of-kin being the main focus, it had been forgotten. By the time they realized that Doctor Peters was attending his wife's and daughter's surgeries, the big issue became whether or not Joshua, as Missy's fiancé, qualified as family. When he was finally allowed to see her, Jasmine had clung to him as to a lifeline. All they'd talked about afterwards was how much to say or not say to Missy and their mother. No one had thought of a possible pregnancy.

As Jasmine lay on the hospital bed, with monitors quietly signaling the continued life within her, she wondered if it would have made any difference if she was pregnant or not. Was the feeling of isolation inside her, this gnawing despair, the result of the pregnancy or the rape? If she had had a chance to work through it at the time and in the days and weeks following, would she still have taken a knife to her body eight months later?

There was now no way of knowing.

She had thought so much about death this past winter.

Maybe she would die giving birth.

JAMIE COULDN'T REMEMBER EVER BEING so angry in her life. Her son's life hanging in the balance—all because of *her*—Jamie couldn't even bear to speak *her* name. And now Andrew's nurse was suggesting that he might be able to rest better if there was just some way to communicate to him that *she* was safe.

The nurse was an older woman with a heavy British accent. She had a tendency to call everyone "dear" and Jamie had the feeling she would just love to solve everyone's problems with a "little cuppa tea."

Jamie, usually open to people from other cultures, found that this woman's accent grated on her nerves.

But everything grated on her nerves right now.

She would give her right arm for her son.

But her right arm was not what he needed…

"He's so restless, poor lad," the nurse prattled on. "You can tell that he's worried about something. He keeps trying to say her name. Is it Jasmine?"

Jamie spoke through gritted teeth, "Yes."

"I think it might be a good idea to get the young lady over here, if she's able. I hear she's a patient here herself…"

With sudden decision, Jamie stood to her feet. *She* would come if Jamie had to drag her by the hair. *She*'d done enough damage. *She* could help for once.

Jamie knew where to find her. She'd be in maternity. That's what this fuss was all about. She didn't have the courage to wait just one more month and give birth to children that deserved to live just as much as she did—possibly even more!

She was lying there so peacefully—as if she didn't have a care in the world.

Jamie grabbed her arm. "C'mon! Andrew needs you."

"Andrew? He's okay? I can see him?"

"No, he's not okay! Thanks to you."

The monitors were beeping. Jamie yanked at the plug. The beeping stopped.

"What—what are you doing?"

"It's just a monitor. It'll just tell you if they're dead or alive—and you weren't so worried about that a few hours ago! You can have them put this back in later, too." Jamie, with many years of nursing experience, removed the IV from Jasmine's arm as well.

The thought flitted through Jamie's mind that she could be charged for this—or at the very least lose her license. It didn't matter. Nothing else mattered right now except the life of her son.

There were no nurses visible in the hallway or at the nurse's station as Jamie hustled her along. Jasmine seemed to falter once, but Jamie held fast to her arm and kept up the pace.

But when she came to a wheelchair folded up against the wall, Jamie opened it and pushed Jasmine down into it. Anything to speed things up.

When they finally got to Andrew's room, he was moving restlessly about. Jamie's eyes flew automatically to the numbers flashing by his bedside, monitoring his vital signs. She moved quickly to his side, felt for his rapid pulse and gently spoke his name. But as before, her presence seemed to have little to no effect.

"Stop crying!" she lashed out at the woman on the opposite side of the bed. "You really think that's going to help him?"

But Jasmine kept crying, her sobs punctuated by words. "Andrew—Andrew—I'm so sorry—"

"That's not what he needs! Can't you stop thinking of yourself for even a minute?"

The old biddy was back—putting her arm around *her*. "He needs your reassurance, love. You've got to let him know that you're all right now."

Her words seemed to calm Jasmine. "Andrew, I'm okay," she said. "Can you hear me? I'm okay." She took his hand. "You need to rest now, Andrew. Just rest…"

She was holding his hand, stroking his forehead.

"You're doing a wonderful job," the nurse gushed. "Such a soft voice you have. And see how much more relaxed he looks."

The nurse was patting *her* on the back. *She* was the one who had hurt him in the first place!

"And you, Mrs. Martin, you look like you could use a nice cuppa tea…"

Jamie stormed out of the room.

She'd go to the cafeteria—*and have a cup of coffee!*

Jasmine felt the pain return.

And she was so thirsty. She thought about drinking some of the water by Andrew's bedside. But what if he woke up and needed it?

When the kind nurse brought her a cup of tea, Jasmine drank it too quickly and it burned all the way down.

"No, no, dearie," she said, patting her hand. "A nice hot cuppa tea is meant to be sipped slowly. Just sit still and I'll get you a nice cold glass of water."

Jasmine nodded and attempted a smile.

When the older woman returned a moment later with a glass of ice water, Jasmine tried to concentrate on drinking it slowly as she watched the nurse take Andrew's vital signs.

"How is he?" Jasmine asked anxiously.

The nurse patted her on the back. "He's doing much better dearie, now that you're here. Well, bless your heart, you *were* thirsty! And now you're trembling like a leaf—maybe we should have just stuck with the nice hot cup of tea. Here, let me get you a housecoat and some slippers." She made a *tsk, tsk* sound as she headed for the door. "Your nurse should have made sure you were dressed properly instead of letting you go off like this."

She came back a moment later and helped Jasmine into the housecoat and slippers, talking all the while. "So what are you in for, dearie? Some kind of surgery you had, by the way you're having difficulty standing…"

"I… yes…" It had been a surgery of sorts—they'd stitched her up and they'd had to use an anesthetic.

"And your poor sweetheart here, too. You were both injured. Were you in an accident together?"

Again Jasmine hesitated. Andrew's injuries were the result of an accident. Hers had been self-inflicted.

Jasmine began a fumbled explanation. "I'm pregnant…"

"Oh, you poor dear," the nurse exclaimed. "And you not looking a day over seventeen."

"I'm eighteen, actually."

The nurse pulled up a chair beside her. "Still far too young, in my opinion. I didn't have my little Emma, God rest her soul, till I was all of twenty-one. And how old is the baby's father, dear?"

She's looking at Andrew!

"He—he's not the—the father."

Jasmine expected reproof and was surprised instead to feel a hand gently squeezing hers.

"Now you just tell me all about it. I'm on my lunch break." She smiled kindly. "But first, tell me where your parents are. They should certainly be with you at a time like this. Maybe I can call them for you, dear."

Jasmine felt a huge ache rising from deep within her, threatening to spill over. *I won't cry! I won't!*

"My mother's dead," she spoke with only a slight tremor in her voice. "And ..." Her head ached with the effort of not crying. "My—my dad is in jail."

"Oh, my dear." The older woman leaned forward and drew Jasmine into a warm hug. Jasmine rested her head on the nurse's shoulder and began to weep. It felt good to just let go—and it felt good to be held and comforted.

But Jasmine pulled away suddenly when she heard Andrew moaning.

She thought she heard him speak her name, but his voice was so faint that she couldn't be sure.

Jasmine moved further away from the nurse, leaning over Andrew instead, speaking softly, telling him that everything was okay. Telling him once again that *she* was okay.

"He's sleeping," the nurse said from beside her.

"Yes," Jasmine whispered softly, watching the gentle rise and fall of his chest. "But I shouldn't be crying. I think maybe he can hear me. And I don't want to upset him."

"Oh, my dear," the older woman said in a tone of rebuke, "if there's one thing I've learned on my journey through life, it's that we all need to cry. Sometimes, the burden gets just too heavy for us to bear."

Jasmine felt pain crashing in around her again ... through her ... all consuming. She wouldn't let it show. She wouldn't!

With gritted teeth, she finally managed to respond, "Yes, but not now. He needs me now."

"It's important that you take care of yourself," the nurse insisted in a kind voice. "If we want to help others, we need to practice good self-care first."

It was like fighting against a giant marshmallow; the more you pushed against it, the more it surrounded you. Soon you wouldn't be able to move—or breathe.

"No!" Jasmine protested. "No, not now. I need to be strong for him. He was strong for me. I need to be strong for him." Jasmine turned away. "And I'd like to be alone with him—please."

"But my dear, I'm only trying to help … "

"Please go," Jasmine pleaded, not daring to look into those kind eyes again—the eyes that pitied her—that would destroy her if she allowed that pity to continually make her feel less than what she was.

"She's right. You need to go. Maybe your lunch break is over now."

Jasmine turned and stared up in surprise at Andrew's mother. *How long has she been there? How much has she heard?*

The nurse stood to her feet and said in an indignant tone, "Well, I'm still the nurse on duty here until three o'clock, so I'll be coming in here for regular checks on my patient … "

Jasmine didn't hear the rest. She was looking in wonder at the transformation in Andrew's mom. It was almost as if she was a different person. She remained standing until the nurse had left the room, then she sat down on the opposite side of the bed from Jasmine. Her smile was one of camaraderie—and pride?

"I'm proud of you," her voice confirmed.

Jasmine was confused. "I know that it's important to cry

sometimes…"

"But it's also important to be strong sometimes," Andrew's mother finished.

"Yes." Jasmine smiled.

Suddenly her smile turned to a wince. The pain was growing again and it was even worse than before!

"Don't hold your breath—go with it. Walk through it. There's nothing to be afraid of… Is it a little better now? Okay…" Andrew's mom looked at her watch and reached for a pen and paper from her handbag. She wrote something down.

Their eyes met. Then Jasmine turned quickly away. She didn't want to know…

"I think maybe you're in labor."

"No, it's just from my stitches. Sometimes they hurt more than at other times."

"If the pain is coming at regular intervals…" Andrew's mom left the sentence unfinished. Her voice was gentle when she spoke. "Just tell me when you feel the pain start to build again."

No! I'm not ready. I'm not ready!

"You're a strong woman."

Jasmine lifted her eyes, soothed by the calm voice.

"And we serve a great God," Andrew's mom continued.

Not me—not for a long time now…

"We'll get through this together."

Jasmine nodded tremulously.

Andrew's mom was looking at her son now, her fingertips resting lightly on his pulse. "He sleeps when you're here." She shook her head. "I don't know if he needs to know that you're okay. Maybe it's just the sound of your voice."

She stood suddenly to her feet. "I need to call obstetrics and tell them you're okay. In the way up on the elevator, they were talking. You—" She lowered her eyes momentarily. "*We*—created a bit of a panic there."

"Mrs. Martin?"

"Yes?"

"It's—it's started again."

Andrew's mom looked at her watch and smiled reassuringly. "Call me Jamie," she said. "Since I'm going to be your labor coach—that is, if you'd like me to be?"

Jasmine could barely nod. The pain was so intense!

"Don't forget to breathe." Jamie's voice came from close beside her. "It's okay. Your body is doing what it's supposed to be doing. Your cervix is stretching—getting ready for the birth."

"I don't want—" Jasmine gasped.

"Shh… shh… It's okay. We'll do this together. And afterwards, too. We'll get you through this—all of it."

Jasmine swiped at the tears in her eyes. "Why twins? *Why?*"

Jamie shook her head. "I don't know," she said gently. "Is it better now? Easing up a little?"

It was. But Jasmine was suddenly afraid. "How many more? And how much worse?"

Jamie took her hand. "I can't tell you that. It's different for every woman. I can just tell you that there *will* be more and it *will* get worse. But we're going to get through this, together."

"Someone needs to be with Andrew…"

"Bill and Kaitlyn will be here soon," Jamie replied. "And you and I can stay here for a while yet, too."

Andrew's nurse strode in at that moment and announced,

"I've just been informed that this patient is supposed to be in obstetrics."

"Yes," Jamie said in a pleasant but equally authoritative voice. "Please let them know that she's here."

"I've already told them that…" the nurse sputtered angrily.

"Then your job is done."

The nurse turned on her heel and marched out.

Less than a minute later, she reappeared with another woman who, by her manner, appeared to be the head nurse.

But Jamie spoke first. "I am a registered nurse. I'm also Jasmine's labor coach. She's doing fine, but we both wish to stay here as long as possible with my son until his father and sister arrive. If I have any concerns at all, I will not hesitate to notify obstetrics immediately."

The head nurse had listened without interruption. She stepped forward and introduced herself. Then she said that she herself would call obstetrics and explain the situation to them.

After both women left, Jasmine turned towards Andrew's mom. "That was great!" she exclaimed. "You are so awesome."

Jamie just shook her head and looked back over at the machines monitoring her son's condition. But Jasmine saw a slow smile begin…

Chapter 10

Jasmine was still in the wheelchair that Jamie had brought her in. As Andrew slept peacefully behind them, his mother helped her into a more comfortable chair. "Try to rest between contractions," she said. "You'll need your strength for later."

Jasmine thanked her. Then they both looked at each other. Something had changed between them.

"What happened?" Jasmine asked. "When you left the room... after refusing the cup of tea?"

Jamie smiled a little sheepishly. "It's called repentance—something Christians do a lot of."

Another contraction came then, making conversation impossible. But after it was over, Jamie gave a fuller answer to Jasmine's question.

"I don't usually get angry, but when I do, I really lose it—as you may have noticed." She smiled wanly before continuing. "When I left here, I stormed my way down to the cafeteria, but it was really crowded and I ended up having to stand in line. There were these two nurses talking in low voices behind me. I heard one of them say, 'At least we know now that he's going to make it.

It was touch and go there for a while.'"

"They were talking about Andrew?" Jasmine asked.

Jamie shook her head. "I'm not actually sure who they were talking about. But suddenly, there in that cafeteria line-up, the Lord spoke to me and said, 'Your son's going to be okay, but what about you?' I had to get out of there quick! It was just like a dam suddenly burst. I made it to the bathroom and then just bawled my eyes out." She looked over at Jasmine and smiled fragilely. "I guess my anger was just grief turned inside out."

Jasmine's smile was one of reassurance. "I think I knew that."

Jamie's voice broke as she whispered, "I thought he was going to die."

Jasmine nodded, unable to speak. *I thought so, too.*

They both looked over at Andrew, and Jasmine allowed herself a moment of pure joy. *He's going to be okay! Andrew's going to be okay!*

Suddenly Jamie flew out of her chair. Jasmine turned in time to see Andrew's father and mother in a tight embrace.

Kaitlyn, Andrew's younger sister, looked around, took in the situation, and came to stand by Jasmine.

"He's sleeping," Jasmine said, trying to sound reassuring.

But Kaitlyn didn't need her reassurance. "My mom's been a nurse for over twenty years. She wouldn't have told my dad that Andrew was going to be okay if he wasn't."

Jasmine could sense the tension in her.

"I would have thought you would be sitting closer to him. You look like you're settled in here as a patient, not a visitor."

Jasmine started to rise, then stopped as a giant fist drove itself into her back.

"You're in labor," Kaitlyn said in an awed voice.

Jasmine couldn't speak—could hardly restrain from crying out.

"I didn't believe them at first. But it's really true. You were pregnant all this time and you kept it from everyone."

Jasmine shut her eyes, wishing she could shut her ears as well.

"I could help you. I learned all about labor and delivery in my health class at school."

"It's okay," Jasmine said through gritted teeth.

"I could get you some ice chips—or—or something."

"No—thanks," Jasmine said, grateful that the pain was easing a bit. She could focus on what was happening around her again.

Andrew's dad was sitting at the bedside with his arm around his wife. Both of them were looking down at Andrew.

"He looks so pale," Andrew's dad spoke in a hoarse whisper.

"He lost a lot of blood," Jamie said. "He'll get some color back in a day or two."

"We almost lost him…"

Jamie squeezed his hand and smiled. "But we didn't."

After a moment, Bill looked back to see where Kaitlyn was. He seemed surprised to find her beside Jasmine.

Or was he surprised to see Jasmine beside Kaitlyn?

"What's she doing here?" Bill asked.

"I asked her—no, I *made* her come. Andrew wouldn't rest until he knew that she was safe."

"Now he knows."

"I'm going to be her labor coach," Jamie said.

Bill spoke sharply. "I would think our son would take priority."

Jamie gently took her husband's hand. "She is our son's priority."

Bill sighed deeply and turned towards Andrew again.

Jamie rubbed his shoulders and Bill reached up and took her hand.

"Can I get you a coffee or something?" Jamie asked.

Bill nodded, his eyes still on Andrew.

"I'll get it, Mom—from the cafeteria?"

"Thanks, Katie, but I can probably get a cup on the floor here. And I need you to do something else for me instead."

Jamie looked at Jasmine as she continued, "Is it okay if Kaitlyn brings you back to your room? I can join you in just a few minutes."

Jasmine felt a brief moment of panic. Jamie was her lifeline. She knew what to do…

"Yes, that will be fine," she said.

Jamie smiled gratefully.

Jasmine, walking over to the wheelchair, was surprised at how weak she felt. It seemed like such an effort but it was really just a few steps.

As Kaitlyn bent to adjust the foot rests, Jasmine took one final look at Andrew. He still seemed to be sleeping. His dad was bent over him, his hand resting on his son's arm. His eyes were closed and his lips were moving. Jamie had sat down beside her husband again, the cup of coffee momentarily forgotten.

Jasmine was barely settled back into her bed, the monitors and IV reinstalled, when another contraction was upon her.

Voices swirled around her, but nothing made sense. Not what the doctor was saying—not what anyone else was saying...

Jasmine took a deep breath as the pain gradually receded once more.

But she was so cold.

She tried to pull the blanket up over her shoulder, but it seemed a huge effort. And she was so thirsty! When had she last had a drink? The nurse had given her tea and then water...

"Ms. Peters..."

Jasmine looked up into the concerned eyes of a nurse. Her doctor appeared to be gone. And Kaitlyn, too.

"How do you feel?"

"Thirsty... and sick... I feel like I might throw up."

"Okay, honey, I'm putting this basin right here for you. You might not actually throw up—you might just feel like it. You shouldn't have anything to drink, but I could get you some ice chips. Are you cold?"

Jasmine nodded and the nurse laid another blanket over her. But she was still cold...

"Jasmine, this is Doctor Ellis. Open your eyes. Tell me how you're feeling."

"I told her..."

"You need to tell me."

"I feel sick—and—and cold..."

And another contraction was coming!

They were getting worse all the time!

No! I can't do it! I can't go through another one!

"Don't fight it. Just breathe. Slowly..."

Jamie!

"Breathe slowly, Jasmine. That's it. That's better. It'll soon be over."

"Are you a friend? Do you know someone we can contact— her parents?"

"Her mother is deceased," Jamie answered. "And her father is—not available. I am a close family friend. I've known Jasmine all her life."

The doctor seemed satisfied. "We're going to perform a Caesarean Section. But we won't be able to do the typical 'bikini' cut and we are planning to use a general anesthetic. Are you following me so far?"

"I'm a registered nurse."

The doctor sounded relieved. "Okay, we think there's some internal bleeding on the upper uterine wall, likely due to the self-inflicted incision. External sutures had been applied previous to the patient being transferred here. Obviously, the attending physician assumed that would be sufficient. Likely it would have been, in other circumstances. But the contractions—"

More voices suddenly appeared in the room.

"Excuse me, Doctor. The blood-work you requested..."

"Yes, of course."

"Jasmine Peters?"

Jasmine opened her eyes and fought against the pain enough to manage a weak reply. "Yes."

"Hi, my name is Devon. I just need to take a little blood from you."

Jasmine felt the needle go in.

"Mom, is there anything I can do?"

Kaitlyn...

"Yeah. If you could call Pastor Thomas. Tell him we need people to be praying. Tell him…" Jamie's voice faded as she walked away.

Another voice sounded close to Jasmine's ear. "Hello, Ms. Peters. My name is Dr. Suben. I will be your anesthesiologist. You are aware that your doctor has ordered a C-Section?"

No! Not another contraction…

Voices swirled around her—lost in a sea of pain.

One rose above the others for a moment. "Ms. Peters, can you hear me? *Ms. Peters!*"

The voice became blurred, fading into a general buzz, then a white wall of silence…

JASMINE… JASMINE!

"Dad! Dad!"

"Andrew! You're awake? How do you feel?"

"Okay. Dad, I—"

"Wait—let me get you some water. You sound like a bull-frog." Bill held a cup with a straw in it and watched as Andrew took a small sip before pulling away again.

"Dad, I—I need to know about Jasmine!"

Bill drew back. "What do you want to know?"

"I can't remember… I must have passed out or something." Andrew's eyes were filled with anxiety. "I don't know if I got the knife away in time. I dreamed that I heard her voice—telling me she was okay. But then, just now—Dad, please tell me!"

"She's okay." Bill controlled his voice with an effort. "She's not the one who got hurt—you were!"

Andrew closed his eyes and sighed. "Thank you, Lord," he

whispered.

Bill stared at his son. Was it really possible that he'd fallen in love with this woman in just four short days? They'd known each other as kids...

Andrew opened his eyes and smiled. "Where am I—the Health Center?"

"No," his father replied. "By the time the doctor got there, you'd already lost a lot of blood. He ordered an air ambulance for you. We..." Bill swallowed hard. "We were really worried about you."

Andrew looked around. "Is Mom here?"

Bill hesitated. "Mom was on the helicopter with you. Katie and I flew down afterwards."

"So Katie and Mom are both here?"

"Yeah, they're here."

Even as he spoke, Bill's mind was racing. He'd have to tell Andrew about Jasmine. But he still looked so pale. And if he really loved the girl...

"Katie and your mom went to help Jasmine," he began cautiously.

"Jasmine! So she *is* here. I thought it was a dream."

Bill sighed deeply. There was no question about it. The guy was head-over-heels in love. The way he was smiling and that faraway look in his eyes.

"So what are they helping Jasmine with?" Andrew asked.

Bill looked away.

"Dad..."

Bill looked at his son and wished he didn't have to be the one to tell him. "Jasmine's pregnant—with twins. And apparently she's already gone into labor."

Andrew groaned and Bill looked away again.

"Where is she?"

Bill turned back quickly at the sound of Andrew's voice. He couldn't remember the last time he'd seen his son cry. Not through all of his teen years, that was for sure.

"Help me up. I've got to go see her. Please!"

Bill put his hands on Andrew's shoulders, but he didn't have to use any force. Andrew was still too weak to move.

"I don't think you should get out of bed yet. We should ask your doctor first. And..." Bill felt way out of his element. Jamie should be here. He pulled some tissues out of the box on the bedside table and handed them clumsily to his son. "It's kind of a woman's domain," he began. "I don't think they would appreciate us being there. Sometimes a husband, but not just friends—or others."

Andrew slowly nodded. "You said that Mom was with her, though—and Katie, too?"

"Yeah, they're both with her. And you know your mom— she's a good nurse. She'll know what to do."

Andrew's eyelids were drooping and Bill was glad he had convinced his son to wait a little while longer before trying to get up.

"I wish I could just see her..."

"She'll be okay," Bill said gently. "And she'll need a friend when all this is over. You won't be able to help much... if you're too sleepy... to even stay awake while your dad's talking to you."

Andrew's eyes were shut. His breathing deep and even.

Bill leaned back in his chair and smiled.

But as he thought about all that Andrew still had to face, Bill closed his eyes and began to pray.

JAMIE HAD LEFT KAITLYN in the waiting room with Missy. They were calling friends and family back home, asking them to pray.

Jamie was anxious to talk to Bill.

The room lights were dim. That was a good sign.

The numbers flashing on Andrew's monitors looked good. And he seemed to be sleeping peacefully. Jamie looked over at Bill and smiled. He was asleep, too.

It had been a long night—and it was turning out to be a long day, too. Jamie yawned. Maybe she would just sit down for a while—and rest her head on the back of this comfortable chair.

"MOM, WAKE UP. It's over."

Jamie opened her eyes and watched as her daughter also quietly woke up her dad. Fortunately, Andrew kept on sleeping.

Kaitlyn motioned for them both to go out into the hallway.

"What's happening?" Bill asked anxiously.

Jamie quickly filled him in. "They had to operate on Jasmine." She turned back toward Kaitlyn, suddenly afraid to ask the question. Jamie had enough medical knowledge to realize that what they were asking for was a miracle. Jasmine might live, or one or both of the babies might live, but it was unlikely all three would.

"They all made it," Kaitlyn spoke quickly, "at least so far. The babies are in Intensive Care and Jasmine is still in Recovery. The doctor told us that we need to keep praying, though. He said that we're not out of the woods yet."

Jamie was surprised to feel tears running down her cheeks. She turned towards Bill. "I wonder if they'd let me in to see the babies."

Bill squeezed her hand. He sounded a little emotional, too. "How much should I tell Andrew when he wakes up again?"

"Again!" Kaitlyn exclaimed.

Now the tears were coming a little faster. Jamie felt as if her heart would burst. "You talked to him?"

Bill nodded and wrapped his arms around her. "He's going to be okay."

"I knew that," Jamie sobbed. "I knew it. I knew he would be okay."

"Now you *really* know it," Bill spoke softly into her hair.

"Can I talk to him?" Kaitlyn asked excitedly.

Jamie pulled away from her husband to turn to her daughter. "He should sleep," she responded automatically, her voice almost steady again. "We should wait for him to wake up on his own."

But Jamie, too, desperately wanted to hear the sound of her son's voice.

They all moved back into his room. Andrew slept on, unaware of his family waiting impatiently for him.

"Mom," Kaitlyn asked after a while, "I'm a little hungry. Would it be all right if I went down to the cafeteria and bought some lunch?"

Lunch? Jamie looked at her watch in surprise—12:40!

Kaitlyn wouldn't have had breakfast either. Jamie picked up her handbag and began rummaging through it. "I should have some money somewhere."

"Maybe I do," Bill offered.

Jamie looked up as her husband pulled out his wallet.

"Uh, sorry honey. I guess I'm out of cash, too."

A low chuckle filled the room. "My parents—perpetually poor."

"Andrew!"

They rushed to his bedside, all three of them speaking at once, asking him how he felt.

Andrew grinned. "Well, I seem to have about as much strength as a cooked spaghetti noodle..."

Kaitlyn giggled while Bill advised, "You just need to give it time."

But Jamie was too overcome to speak. She just put her arms around her son and wept.

Chapter 11

"AND HOW'S JASMINE? Has she had the babies yet?"

Jamie's silence was not what he had expected. She scrambled for the right words to say. "Yes..."

"Mom, what's wrong?" Andrew asked anxiously. "Is there something wrong with one of the babies?"

Jamie was surprised that he even knew about the pregnancy—and he'd said *babies*—plural.

"You knew that Jasmine was expecting twins?"

"Dad told me—before you guys came. Are they all right?" he asked impatiently. "And you would have told me if something had happened to Jasmine..."

There was guilty silence for just a fraction of a second too long.

"Where is she?" he demanded. "What happened to her? Why didn't you tell me right away?"

"She's in the recovery room," Jamie spoke quickly. "And she's probably going to be okay."

"*Probably!* What's that supposed to mean?"

He was trying to pull himself up, but didn't have the strength.

Bill gently pushed him back down again. "It means she has a really good chance," he said.

"You've gotta—help me," Andrew spoke, breathless from his efforts. "I've gotta—see her."

"She's in the recovery room," Jamie spoke practically. "They won't let you visit there. If there's any change, Missy will let us know." Jamie looked at her son's anxious face. "But maybe I could go down and ask…"

"I'll go, Mom." Kaitlyn hurried out of the room.

"You keep saying the recovery room," Andrew said in a worried voice. "I thought women just went to delivery rooms. And they can have visitors…"

"She had an operation," Jamie interjected.

"Why?" Andrew's eyes were fearful. "Did they find something wrong with the babies? Are you saying that she had a C-section?"

Jamie sighed. "There was some internal bleeding—from the knife wound."

Andrew was trying to sit up again. "But I got there in time. She was here—wasn't she? I heard her. Dad said—"

"She was here." Bill put his hands on Andrew's shoulders again and kept them there.

"But…" Andrew looked from one of them to the other. "She said she was okay. I remember she said that—didn't she?"

"Yes," Jamie quickly assured him. "But there was some internal bleeding and when she started having contractions, it got worse."

"And the babies?"

"They're in the Intensive Care Nursery."

"Why?" Andrew's voice trembled. "Why are they there? The—the knife?"

"No!" Jamie, too, was appalled by the thought. "No, I'm quite sure they are just premature. I was going to go down and see."

Andrew shook his head. "I need to go." He looked up at Bill. "Please..."

His father slowly nodded.

"You'll need to get your doctor's permission," Jamie protested. "If he thinks you're stable enough... These monitors..."

But Andrew was already pulling off the little circles of tape with their connecting wires. A loud beeping filled the room.

Jamie had to smile. *Like mother, like son.*

"What's going on here? He can't do that! Stop him!"

Jamie and Bill exchanged glances as the nurse continued her tirade. "I'll call the head nurse. I'll—I'll call the doctor," she sputtered.

As the irate woman left the room, Bill winked at Jamie. "Do you think we could have him out of here before she gets back?"

Hmm... Maybe it was like father, like son, too.

Jamie hurried towards the door. She'd have to find a wheelchair.

"Leave the IV in," she called over her shoulder to them.

Fortunately, there was a wheelchair out in the hallway. Jamie spied out the land while she was at it. If they could get to the elevator undetected...

Andrew was sitting up on the edge of his bed, but leaning heavily on Bill. Jamie stopped. Maybe they weren't doing the right thing...

But the moment Andrew saw her, he pulled himself upright.

Jamie saw the determination in his eyes and in that moment, he realized that the choice was really not hers to make.

The IV monitor was battery operated and on wheels. Jamie pushed it along in pace with Bill, who guided the wheelchair down the hall.

The strident voice of Andrew's nurse reached their ears just as the elevator door closed. "You can't—!"

But we did.

Jamie looked carefully at Andrew. "How do you feel?" she asked.

Bill kept a hand on his son's shoulders as the elevator lurched to a stop.

"I'm okay," Andrew answered.

"Not dizzy? Not nauseated? Not thirsty?" Jamie persisted.

"I am a little thirsty," Andrew admitted.

Jamie made Bill stop the wheelchair as she bent to take Andrew's pulse.

"Hey, you're up!" Kaitlyn's voice sounded from above them. "You can see the babies through the window," she said, "but Jasmine's still in Recovery."

His pulse was strong and steady. "How thirsty are you?" Jamie persisted.

"Katie, could you find Andrew a glass of water or some juice?" Bill directed. "Maybe ask a nurse or go down to the cafeteria. We'll be at the nursery, honey."

Bill smiled reassuringly at Jamie.

She kept a watchful eye on Andrew as they continued, but he did seem to be tolerating the trip well enough.

When they asked to see the babies, the nurse hesitated. She

looked at each of them before settling her attention on Andrew. "Are you the father?"

Jamie watched in amazement as Andrew, after only a slight hesitation, nodded his head. "Yes, I am."

Jamie grabbed Bill's hand. Andrew would never lie. Maybe he'd gone down to visit her in the States…

"We don't have the same last name yet…" Andrew's voice faded as the nursery door closed behind him.

"Bill…" Jamie couldn't keep the fear from her voice.

But her husband seemed unconcerned. "He loves her. I assume she loves him. It's not too much of a stretch to think he might be planning to adopt her children."

"It's just all going too fast!"

Bill chuckled. "Just because it took us about ten years to figure out that we loved each other."

Jamie smiled at him, relaxing a little. "We were just children. We had to grow up first."

Bill put his arm around her. "Yeah, and then when you were finally all grown up, you fell in love with Jeff," he teased.

"It wasn't really love," Jamie said, looking into his eyes. "What I have for you…"

Bill took her in his arms. "I know."

Jamie kissed him and then pulled away a little. "Do you think he's already asked her?"

Bill didn't answer for a moment. He was looking through the nursery window. Andrew had put a gown on top of his hospital pajamas and housecoat.

"I don't suppose there's been time," Bill said thoughtfully.

"But isn't he assuming too much?" Jamie asked as they

watched the nurse hand Andrew one of Jasmine's babies.

A cloud of fluffy brown hair was just visible above the pink blanket. Andrew looked up at that moment and saw them standing there. His face broke into a broad smile. He held the baby up for them to see.

Jamie's eyes blurred with tears. She wiped impatiently at them, berating herself. *I'm not usually this weepy.*

Bill chuckled softly as he stood behind her, his arms wrapped around Jamie's waist. "Grandmas are allowed to cry," he said softly.

They continued to watch as the nurse took the baby from Andrew and placed her back into the incubator. Then she wheeled him over to the second one. This baby must not be doing as well.

Andrew's face was grave as he reached in through the arm-holes of the incubator and gently touched the baby lying spread-eagle on the white sheet, wires and tubes seemingly attached to every possible place on the tiny body.

Jamie, watching him, thought her heart would break.

"That's the little one we still need to be praying for," Bill said.

Jamie nodded silently.

Kaitlyn arrived at that moment. "Had to go to the cafeteria," she said, her words coming in a rush. "Got there. Realized I had no money. Had to go borrow some from Missy. She wanted to know if I knew how Andrew was and, of course, I wanted to know how Jasmine was—"

"How is she?" Jamie interjected.

"Well, she's still in the recovery room, I know that," Kaitlyn replied in a slower, more thoughtful voice. "But Missy said the doctor told her that Jasmine's condition had 'stabilized'—I think that was the word he used—but that they still wanted to keep her in a bit longer for 'observation'."

Jamie looked at her watch. "It's been almost an hour. That's a long time in Recovery. And they don't know when she'll be up on the floor?"

"No, I don't think so," Kaitlyn spoke hesitantly. "Do you want me to go back up and ask?"

Jamie looked through the nursery window. Andrew still had his arm in the incubator. He was talking to the baby—or perhaps praying.

Jamie turned back to her daughter. "Yeah, if you don't mind going back, honey. Andrew will want to know."

Kaitlyn smiled. "I don't mind. Here's Andrew's juice. Should I get you guys something?"

"I could use a coffee," Jamie said.

Bill reached for his wallet. "Here, take my card. I think I saw a money machine on the way in. Get out sixty—no, make it a hundred. Then we'll have it when we need it. And did you eat yet?"

"No, do you want me to get something for all of us?"

Jamie noticed that the nurse was wheeling Andrew away from the incubator now. Jamie caught a glimpse of his face. He looked worn-out, physically and emotionally.

"Yeah, maybe some sandwiches," Bill answered distractedly, his eyes on Andrew as well.

"We'll probably be up in Andrew's room by the time you come back." Jamie turned to give her daughter a hug. "Thank you for being such a big help."

Kaitlyn grinned. "Hey, no problem!"

Bill turned to hug her as well. "Thanks, Katie."

The nurse was pushing Andrew through the connecting doors. Jamie hurried to meet him. Bill was beside her as the nurse said in a concerned voice, "Your son really needs some rest."

"We'll bring him down to his room right away," Bill promised.

Andrew lifted his head. "But what about Jasmine?"

Jamie knelt down beside him, her fingers automatically going to his pulse. "She's still in Recovery; Katie's keeping us posted on her progress."

Andrew looked up at the nurse. "I'll be back later. Let me know if there's any change in Amy's condition."

Amy! Jamie groaned inwardly—Andrew had named them already!

She rose slowly to her feet, thankful that her husband was there with them—calm, easygoing Bill. "Yes, please keep us posted," he said. "Do you have Andrew's room number?"

Jamie watched the nurse nod as Bill took the handles of the wheelchair from her. Both Bill and Andrew expressed their thanks, but Jamie was still too much in shock to reply. She feared her son was getting in way over his head!

Andrew's nurse met them in the hallway and there was little opportunity for conversation until he was properly settled back into bed, the monitors once more flashing out their reassuring numbers.

Jamie hesitated, knowing he needed to sleep, but feeling it was imperative that she say something.

"Andrew…"

The weariness in his eyes drove all thoughts of conversation from her mind. "Nothing," she said. "You rest now. We'll be here if you need us."

Andrew closed his eyes again.

When Kaitlyn returned a few minutes later, they quickly ushered her out of the room, afraid that their talking might wake Andrew.

"How is she?" Jamie asked when they were out in the hallway.

"It's awful, Mom. They put her in this room with this other lady who has her baby with her. All her family's there oogling and googling over the new baby. Jasmine's got her curtains drawn, but it doesn't help much."

"We can get her moved," Jamie said.

"Missy's been trying to do that," Kaitlyn replied. "People aren't being very sympathetic towards Jasmine. They don't really know—the whole story."

Jamie was actually a little surprised that her daughter knew it! But then, she'd spent most of the day with Missy. "Is Joshua here yet?" she asked.

"No, but he's on his way—and so is Rosalee. Michael's going to stay and take care of things at the lodge and keep the fire going at the Peters' house."

"How is Missy doing?" Jamie asked.

Kaitlyn shook her head. "Not that good. I think everything's finally getting to her—about her dad and now her sister."

"Maybe I should go up there," Jamie mused.

"Just take a minute and eat first," Bill suggested. "And maybe we should all pray together before you go, too."

After they'd eaten and each of them had prayed, Jamie left Bill and Kaitlyn to watch over Andrew as she headed upstairs to see Jasmine.

There did seem to be a party atmosphere in the double room that Jasmine was sharing with another woman. Several people were visiting the new mother and her baby, taking pictures, opening gifts, talking, and laughing. Their happiness was evident as they greeted Jamie. Everyone was a friend on their joyous day.

If Jasmine had aborted the babies, or if they had died following birth, she wouldn't have been placed in the same room as this new mother. But Jasmine's twins were alive—and there had been no preplanned adoption. There should have been someone—her doctor, perhaps—who knew about the self-inflicted knife wounds. But as Kaitlyn had said, perhaps there were only a very few who knew the whole story. Jasmine hadn't succeeded in aborting her children—but she had wanted to.

Jamie parted the curtains and came upon a very different scene from the one in the other half of the room.

Jasmine was lying motionless on the bed, her eyes fixed in a blank stare, a steady stream of tears flowing from her eyes.

Missy, sitting on a chair beside her, looked both physically— and emotionally—exhausted.

"How're you guys doing?" Jamie asked in a gentle voice.

Missy shook her head wearily. "She's been like this ever since they brought her in here."

Jamie glanced at the numbers on the monitors surrounding Jasmine. She was doing okay physically...

"And the nurses said she cried the whole time in the recovery room," Missy continued in a voice that was strained with grief and fatigue.

"Honey, why don't you go take a break?" Jamie suggested. "I'll sit with her a while."

Missy looked doubtful and Jamie felt a stab of shame. Missy was right to mistrust her after all the terrible things she'd said and done. "I was angry," Jamie said in a quiet voice. "All that I could think about right then was my son."

Missy stood to her feet. "I do need to use the bathroom—and maybe get a drink or something. Just please don't do anything to upset her—any more than she already is." Missy's voice trailed off as she looked down at her sister. Then she turned and walked resolutely into the midst of the celebration that was unwittingly causing so much pain.

Chapter 12

ANDREW SLEPT FOR A LITTLE OVER AN HOUR and awoke refreshed—and hungry. A new nurse was on duty—a young man named Matt, who was about Andrew's age and just newly graduated from college.

Matt advised Andrew to take it slow on the food, perhaps starting with some soup or Jell-O to begin with. Andrew's doctor came in to see him while he was eating. Hearing of Andrew's trip to the nursery, he smiled benignly and said that they might as well remove the monitors. But he did still want to keep the IV in—at least for the time being.

He gave Andrew a thorough examination and said that there didn't appear to be any signs of internal or external bleeding. "I guess we pretty much got you patched up," he said. "And if your stitches held this afternoon with all that gallivanting around the hospital you did—" He patted Andrew on the shoulder and smiled kindly. "Just listen to your body," he advised. "If you're tired, sleep. If you're hungry, eat. That sort of thing. Try walking when you feel you're ready."

After the doctor left, Andrew did try walking. He made it to the bathroom and back holding onto his father's arm for support, but the short trip left him feeling tired and sore; he knew he couldn't walk any kind of distance on his own yet.

But he was extremely anxious to go and see Jasmine. Kaitlyn had told him about Jasmine's room situation and Andrew hoped that by the time he got down there, his mom would have managed to get her transferred to a private room.

His dad and Kaitlyn went with him, pushing Andrew's wheelchair and IV pole. There was a woman with a cart of flowers on the elevator when they stepped on and she got off at the same floor they did. She stopped at Jasmine's room and smiled as she saw that they were stopping also. "Lots of flowers for this room," she said in a bubbly voice.

His dad and Kaitlyn were pushing him past, but Andrew put out his hand to stop them. "Wait," he said to the woman. "Where can I get some of those?"

She smiled warmly at him. "Downstairs at the gift shop, dear." The woman picked up a large flower arrangement in one hand and a fruit basket in the other. "My goodness, this must be one special lady!"

"Yes, she is," Andrew said, swallowing back the ache in his voice. He'd make sure Jasmine got the biggest bunch of flowers they had—and fruit—and Teddy bears—and whatever else was down there at that shop.

It was like suddenly being thrust from a party into a funeral.

His mom looked up as they entered, but she seemed at a loss for words. Jasmine was staring vacantly up at the ceiling. Her eyes were red from crying and still moist from freshly fallen tears.

Andrew's mother moved away from the side of the bed,

taking her chair with her so that his dad could push him in closer to Jasmine.

But Andrew, too, found himself with nothing to say. It was as if there was a thick wall of pain sealing her off, separating her from the rest of the world.

He touched her tentatively on the shoulder. "Jasmine..." he whispered, forcing the words past the lump in his throat.

There was no change—no indication that she'd even heard him.

With a groan, Andrew leaned forward in his wheelchair, took her face in his hands, looked into her glazed eyes and spoke her name with all the intensity in his heart.

The sudden sharp pain he saw reflected in her eyes made him wish for a moment that he'd allowed her to remain numb. But he knew there could be no comfort, no easing of the pain until it was acknowledged and shared with another. "Jasmine," he said gently as he moved his hands down to clasp hers, "you're not alone. We're going to get through this together."

Her lips trembled and tears filled her eyes. When she spoke, it was a breathless cry, weak and vulnerable as a child's. "They're alive..."

The words tore through his heart. *Yes, and they're beautiful,* Andrew longed to tell her. Instead, he bowed his head over their joined hands—and wept.

He'd been praying silently for some time before becoming consciously aware of it—his heart crying out to God on behalf of Jasmine—and the two little babies, Ashley and Amy.

Her hands felt warm and relaxed in his. Andrew looked up, and with a sense of wonder and gratitude realized that Jasmine had fallen asleep. He glanced around. His family was gone. Even the people in the other part of the room seemed to have quieted down.

Andrew, afraid that Jasmine might wake up again, was reluctant to move. But he was getting very tired. It was so frustrating to be this weak at a time when Jasmine needed him to be strong.

His mother walked quietly into the room at that moment and her eyes filled with concern when she saw him. Andrew attempted a smile and nodded faintly. *Yes, I am ready to go back…*

Carefully he released his hold on Jasmine's hands, watching to be sure that her breathing remained deep and even before moving further. Satisfied that she was still asleep, Andrew allowed himself to be wheeled away from her.

The woman in the other bed was asleep, her round of visitors finally gone. Her baby was asleep as well, in a portable crib beside her. Flowers and gifts covered every conceivable space. Andrew determined once again that, at the earliest possible moment, he would order something for Jasmine.

Kaitlyn met them at the door. "I'll stay with her," she volunteered.

As Andrew's mother pushed him back to his room, she talked to him, but most of her words seemed to just float past, fatigue making it difficult for him to take in what she was saying. Something about his dad… gone to book hotel rooms. And Joshua and Rosalee here now… wanting to see him…

"Too tired…" he murmured as his mom and the nurse lifted him out of the wheelchair and back into bed.

He was about to surrender to sleep when he forced himself awake again. "I don't want to sleep too long—please." He struggled to form the words. "If Jasmine wakes up... And they said they'd tell me how Amy's doing... And Ashley... I want... to see... Ash..."

JASMINE COULD HEAR MISSY and Joshua arguing.

Missy sounded way, way past tired! Too far gone to listen to anything logical that Joshua was trying to tell her. "I can't just leave her!" Missy argued.

"She wouldn't be alone," Joshua responded. "Kaitlyn and Jamie are here. And as soon as I get you settled in at the hotel for the night, I'll come right back here too, if you want."

Missy sounded weepy. "What if she wakes up?"

"She's been sleeping for almost two hours. She'll probably sleep right through the night."

Not if you two guys keep arguing.

Jasmine kept her eyes shut, too weary to bother opening them. Missy would stay—or Missy would go. It didn't really matter. Nothing did.

"What do you think you're doing!" Missy suddenly screamed.

Jasmine opened her eyes. Andrew was there in a wheelchair with his dad standing behind him. In Andrew's arms...

Jasmine tried to look away—tried hard not to think about it.

But everything within her was calling out for... her child, her baby. A girl probably, wrapped in a pink blanket... Her hair just a little lighter than Andrew's; her complexion almost the same. So beautiful. So perfect. So innocent.

Missy was still yelling. Joshua was trying to calm her down. People were moving about. Jasmine could hear it all, but it didn't really reach her. There was just her and her baby—and Andrew. Jasmine glanced up. Their eyes met.

Andrew was holding the baby cradled in one arm. He grabbed onto the bed and pulled himself closer with his free hand.

They were very close now. She could reach out and touch them.

"I was going to wait," Andrew said gently. "I didn't know if you were ready. I didn't even know if you'd be awake. But they brought her in to see me—and I just had to show you. She's so beautiful. I—I hope you don't mind that I named her," he continued nervously. "It just didn't seem quite right for her not to have a name."

Jasmine nodded, tears brimming in her eyes. She wiped them away, not wanting anything to blur her vision.

"You could always change it later. It's not like it's really official or anything. It's just that—"

"Andrew…" She reached out to touch his hand.

"No, that's a boy's name," Andrew babbled. "Her name is Ashley and her sister is Amy." Andrew moved her closer. Now the bottom of her blanket touched their joined hands. "She's the biggest so she has the biggest name. Amy is smaller. She had a rough start, but the doctor said she's going to be okay now. They're identical twins and it might be hard to tell them apart at first, but if we just remember that Ashley is the big one—"

"With the big name." Jasmine couldn't help smiling.

It was just a matter of inches to move her hand up. But Jasmine knew with every ounce of her being that as she touched the soft skin and downy hair, she wasn't traveling inches but miles—and years. It was a journey she was ready to begin…

"Uh, Jasmine…" Jamie's voice broke in. "We're just going to head out now. We'll see you tomorrow, okay?"

Jasmine looked up and smiled at her family—hers and Andrew's. They were standing together at the foot of her bed, all of them looking a little teary-eyed. Jasmine was grateful to them for allowing her the time and space that she needed.

"Thank you," Andrew spoke for both of them.

"You can press on the buzzer and one of the nurses will bring you back."

Andrew nodded in response to his dad's suggestion and, with parting smiles and a blown kiss from Katie, their families left for the night.

The enormity of what they were doing suddenly struck Jasmine. "Andrew," she whispered, "are you really sure about all this?"

He smiled broadly. "As sure as I've ever been." The baby moved in his arms. "Hey, look who's waking up."

Ashley gave them a big yawn and began to wiggle out of her blanket. One hand popped out, followed almost immediately by the other.

Jasmine and Andrew laughed and each held out a finger for her to grasp.

"She's got a good strong grip," Andrew said.

Jasmine felt the tiny fingers not only clasping her hand but her heart as well. "And she's so beautiful."

"Just like her mommy," Andrew spoke softly.

Ashley proceeded to free up her feet as well.

"Kicking off your blanket," Andrew chided. "Just like your daddy."

Andrew heard Jasmine gasp and looked up. Her face had lost all its color.

"Like me," Andrew spoke quickly. "I meant me. I kick off the covers all the time."

But Jasmine just stared at him. "This—this isn't some game," she said in a tightly controlled voice. "We're not playing house."

ANDREW FELT AS IF A GIANT FIST had sunk deep into his chest, crushing each rib. "I would never do that to you," he said.

She looked intently at him, as if searching his eyes for the truth. "You said 'daddy'," she finally spoke, her voice a fragile whisper.

Andrew could feel Ashley wiggling in his arms. He glanced down at her. She was working herself up for a good cry. Andrew reached into the bag the nursery had provided for him, got out the baby pacifier, and popped it into her mouth before drawing the blankets tightly around her again. She liked to be held up against his shoulder and have her back rubbed.

As Andrew lifted Ashley up, he noticed that Jasmine was still gazing intently at him. The baby rested her head on his shoulder, her face turned in towards his neck. She made soft, sucking sounds on the soother as he rubbed her back with slow, circular motions. "Yes, I said 'daddy'."

"You—" Her throat seemed to close around the word,

making it sound as if she were choking. "You seem…" she tried again, this time with more success. "You seem to be forgetting something."

But Ashley was starting to fuss again. Something was wrong—something that couldn't be fixed by a soother or a back rub. "Maybe she needs her diaper changed," Andrew mused aloud. He took a diaper out of the bag the nursery had given him. Now he'd have to lay her somewhere flat. He'd watched the nurse do this—it didn't look too hard.

There was room at the end of the bed. "Just don't move your feet," he cautioned Jasmine.

Oh no, he hadn't been prepared for this! The diaper wasn't just wet…

Maybe there were some of those wet cloth thingies in the bag, too. Whew! There was. Now if he just held both her feet with one hand—and if she didn't wiggle around too much…

"Andrew!"

Couldn't she see he was busy! "Yes," he answered, wondering what to do with the messy diaper and cloths.

"You haven't heard a word I've said, have you?"

"Uh, yeah, I think so. Hey, what do I do with all this?"

At least she was smiling a little now. "Just fold it again with the dirty diaper wipes inside. Then roll it up and use one of the sticky tabs to hold it closed. Then you throw it away. Here, there's a bag by my table."

Andrew slid a clean diaper under the baby's bottom. Voices sounded from the other side of the curtain. Jasmine's roommate was back. Andrew hadn't appreciated how quiet it was until it was noisy again.

"Actually the tabs go on the bottom," Jasmine said. "They fold forward over the front of the diaper."

Andrew moved the diaper to the correct position, flipped up the front of it, and attached first one tab and then the other. It looked okay…

"It'll need to be a bit tighter or it'll fall off," Jasmine advised.

The voices on the other side of the room were gone. But someone was still moving around. Maybe she was moving out, Andrew thought hopefully.

Andrew readjusted the tabs, pulling the diaper a little tighter to make a snug fit. "There now," he said to Ashley as she met his gaze once more. "That feels better, doesn't it? Oh, but your nightgown is all wet, too. What are we going to do about that?"

There weren't any fresh clothes in the bag. Andrew glanced around in frustration. "She needs some clothes…"

Andrew immediately regretted his comment as Jasmine spoke in a fretful voice. "Usually… uh, normally… women pack… they've already bought…"

"Hey, you guys, I don't mean to be eavesdropping…" a cheerful voice began.

Andrew groaned inwardly. *Jasmine's roommate…*

"It's just that I got way more clothes given to me for Karyn than I could possibly use." The woman had a pile of baby clothes in her hands. "Did you know you were going to have twins?"

"No," Jasmine managed in a barely audible voice.

"And then for them to come early…" Jasmine's roommate took a step closer, moving across the invisible divider between the two halves of their room. "And I hear that you had to have a C-Section, too. I feel kind of guilty that my birth was so easy compared to yours." She set the clothes down on the end of the bed. "You guys look like you're busy," she said, the words coming out in a rush. "I didn't mean to interrupt. It's just that I'll be leaving soon. The doctor was going to release me tomorrow morning, but I asked if I could go home tonight so my husband wouldn't have to take time off work…" Her voice trailed away as she stepped back.

She had already moved to the other side of the curtain when Andrew found his tongue at last. "Wait!" he called in a breathless voice.

She appeared again, looking mildly surprised.

"I just wanted to thank you. We do appreciate it. Maybe we could pay you or something…"

The woman's face broke into a smile. "No, no, it's fine," she said. "And I'd like to leave at least one of these flower arrangements with you, too. I have so many."

Andrew, still feeling a little overwhelmed, could only nod his thanks.

"Thank you," Jasmine spoke suddenly from behind him.

"You're welcome." The young woman smiled graciously before turning to go back to her packing.

Ashley was starting to fuss again. She was probably cold. Andrew looked at the pile of clothes. He'd never dressed a baby before either. He picked up the top garment—a soft, white, one-piece thing with a zipper on the front.

He'd managed to get Ashley's legs into it and was about to put an arm through when he suddenly noticed the words embroidered on it—"Daddy's Girl."

Andrew glanced up at Jasmine. "It says——"

"I know," she said quickly. "It's——it's perfect."

Chapter 13

ANDREW FINISHED DRESSING ASHLEY and wrapped her in the blanket as well. "There's a bottle too, I think," he said, reaching down into the bag once more.

It looked like it just had water in it, but the baby took to it readily enough. And she seemed to be falling asleep again.

Jasmine's roommate stepped around the curtain to say a quick goodbye, leaving behind a large arrangement filled with roses, daisies, and carnations.

Andrew thanked her again. He heard her leave and was thankful once again for the silence—and the privacy.

Andrew eased the bottle away. Ashley was fast asleep.

Suddenly he remembered that Jasmine had been trying to tell him something.

He glanced up at her. Her eyes were on Ashley—watching her sleep.

It had been just after Andrew had said the word "daddy." Jasmine had told him that he was forgetting something…

"Oh man!" Andrew groaned.

Jasmine's eyes filled with alarm. "What?"

"Did I ever ask you to marry me?" he demanded.

"Um, no," she replied in a breathless voice.

Andrew shook his head, angry with himself. "Did I ever even tell you that I loved you?"

"No, but you *have* shown me."

"Yeah, but I should tell you these things! Girls like to hear that kind of stuff, don't they?"

Jasmine's eyebrows arched. "*That kind of stuff?*"

Andrew rubbed his forehead. He needed to lie down again soon.

And the atmosphere was all wrong, he knew that much at least. "There should be candles and music and a nice dinner or something—and a ring—I should have a ring—"

"Andrew…" Her voice was filled with love *for him!*

And when he looked into her eyes, they were dancing with light. Laughing, teasing eyes—just like he remembered.

"You still haven't asked me."

Andrew swallowed past the lump in his throat and spoke the words that were in his heart. "I love you, Jasmine." He spoke the words as a vow. "I want to be your husband and the father of your children. Will you marry me?"

"Yes."

"Yes?" Andrew felt a brief moment of panic, quickly replaced by a truckload of joy. "You mean it? You really will? Like soon, or in a month or two or—?"

Jasmine laughed—a bubbling kind of sound that he hadn't heard in a long time. It felt good to hear it now.

"We can talk about which day would be best," she said. "But the answer is yes—unequivocally, irrevocably, unconditionally…"

Andrew rolled his eyes.

"Hey, you do that almost as good as Katie!"

Andrew laughed. Ashley stirred in his arms. He stroked her cheek. "Hey, you taking notes?" he asked tenderly. "I'm going to be your daddy—officially—and unequivocally—and irrevocably."

Their laughter flowed and blended and became as one. Andrew leaned forward to kiss Jasmine—and felt a wave of dizziness come over him. He pulled back with a low groan.

"Are you okay?" Jasmine quickly asked.

"Just tired," he said.

"Maybe I should take Ashley."

Andrew readily agreed.

Jasmine turned her shoulders slightly so that Ashley fit into the crook of her arm. The little girl seemed content to be there— safe in her mother's arms.

Tears sprang suddenly to Jasmine's eyes. "I almost killed her," she whispered hoarsely.

The memory of that moment flashed back vividly in Andrew's mind.

When he'd seen her there on the floor with the knife in her hand—and blood staining her shirt…

"Don't think about that now," he said quickly. "It's in the past. We have the future ahead of us to look forward to."

But Jasmine was shaking her head. "I need to face the truth in my life—all of it. I've been running and hiding too long. I've shut people out and I've hurt them—and myself—in the process. I kept saying I wanted to be alone." Her voice trailed off to a whisper. "But I didn't really…"

Andrew squeezed her hand. "You're not alone anymore."

Jasmine smiled wanly. "I know—and I can't tell you how much your love means to me. It's everything…" She shook her head and looked away. "Almost everything…"

Andrew's heart was beating like a jackhammer. *What more could she possibly have to tell me?*

"I've been angry with God…"

Andrew's heart slowed to a more reasonable rate. He'd known—or at least had guessed as much.

"It's one thing to feel cut off from my family and friends—but to feel cut off from God, too—"

"He's been right here waiting for you," Andrew said softly. "You know He promised to never leave us nor forsake us."

Jasmine drew in a shaky breath. Her eyes were on Ashley. "Though a mother may forsake her—" Jasmine's voice broke into a sob.

Andrew gently stroked her cheek. He knew what verse she was thinking of. "Can a mother forget the baby at her breast and have no compassion on the child she has borne? Though she may forget, I will never forget you! See, I have engraved you on the palms of my hands; your walls are ever before me." He smiled at Jasmine. "Isaiah 49:15-16."

She gave him a wan smile in return. "Maybe you should have been a preacher instead of a cop."

"No, not me. It's just that I've been thinking about that verse a lot lately."

Jasmine bowed her head.

Andrew gently raised her chin. "As a reminder of God's love," he said.

Jasmine blinked back the tears and tried to smile.

"And you know…" Andrew began excitedly, his hand falling to rest on top of Jasmine's. "It's really neat if you look at the words carefully."

Jasmine's smile grew wider.

"No, listen," he said, "this is really cool. I always thought that it said that God had carved us on the palm—singular—of his hand—singular. But what it actually says is that he carved us on the *palms* of his *hands*."

"It makes a difference?" Jasmine asked.

"Yeah, it sure does. Like, let's say I'm God, right…"

"Well…" Jasmine teased.

Andrew grinned and continued with his "sermon."

"Okay, so here's you carved on the *palm* of my *hand*. But being God, I'm pretty busy…" Andrew moved his arm around. Sometimes his hand was up or down or sideways.

Jasmine watched his hand moving around, her eyebrows raised a little, an amused smile on her lips.

"Okay," Andrew continued in a softer voice, "this is you carved on the *palms* of my *hands*." Andrew cupped his hands together and brought them up to eye level in front of his face. "And your walls are ever before me. Walls in the Bible always mean protection. See…" Andrew turned his cupped hands towards her. "The walls are God's hands—just like a cradle. And…" He moved his hands back so they were facing towards him again. "Your walls are ever before me. It's like you're just right there…"

Jasmine bit her lip, once more fighting back the tears.

"I'm not the only one who loves you," Andrew said gently.

Jasmine nodded. "I know," she whispered.

Andrew felt a wave of fatigue wash over him once more. He knew that he wouldn't be able to remain upright for very much longer. "I've got to go."

Jasmine smiled at him tenderly. "Thank you for being here— for me—and for Ashley—and for Amy. Do—do you think they'd let me go see her?"

"I *know* they would," Andrew said.

He pressed the buzzer for a nurse. He needed to get back to his room and lie down. The nurse could bring Ashley back to the nursery if and when Jasmine was ready for that. They were both looking pretty cozy at the moment.

"Andrew..."

"Mmm?"

He'd been resting his head on his hand, his bent elbow on the arm of the wheelchair. Reluctantly, he opened his eyes.

"Andrew, did Joshua ever mention to you something about a seven-week program he was doing?"

Andrew lifted his head. "Yes, they're starting one this Wednesday. Today is... Actually I have no idea what day today is!"

A low chuckle came from behind him. "It's Sunday—the Lord's day. But it's just about over—and you kids look like you're about done in, too."

Andrew turned. A tall man with dark skin and darker hair stood by the foot of the bed. He reminded Andrew a little of Jasmine's grandfather, Tom Peters.

"Nurse told me you might be needin' a ride to the surgical

floor. I's going that way myself. Thought I might give you a hand."

"Thanks," Andrew said, touched by the man's kindness. He turned towards Jasmine. "I'll see you tomorrow, then."

He looked up at the tall man, noticing for the first time that he was wearing a surgical suit. His tag read: Dr. Israel Jones.

The doctor followed his gaze. "Emergency appendectomy," he explained with a wide smile. "I'm not usually wandering the halls at this time of the night."

"You shouldn't go out of your way—"

"Like I said, I's headin' that way anyhow."

Andrew knew he should hurry. But still he hesitated.

The doctor seemed to read his mind. "Oh, go ahead and kiss her goodnight. I'll turn my back," he quipped.

Andrew felt the color rise in his face. He bent quickly to kiss Jasmine on the cheek. She turned her head and the kiss fell on her lips. Andrew's heart did a series of cartwheels and he leaned forward to kiss her again.

"All right! All right! A goodnight kiss is one thing…" The older man chuckled. "But I got my own wife to get home to."

Andrew gave Jasmine a quicker kiss than he would have liked. He kissed Ashley gently on the forehead as well. "Goodnight, princess," he told the sleeping baby.

The doctor had moved around behind Andrew. "Ready to go?" he asked, beginning already to push Andrew forward a little.

"Yeah, I'm ready," Andrew said, unable to resist one last glance as they turned to leave the room.

THE NEXT THREE DAYS PASSED QUICKLY. Ashley was doing well enough to be moved into Jasmine's room and the doctor was saying that perhaps they could all go home soon if Amy could be transferred to the Rabbit Lake Health Centre. They had surprisingly good neonatal facilities there—a legacy of Rachel's Children.

Andrew was finally able to buy Jasmine the flowers he'd wanted and these were soon joined by a multitude of cards and gifts from other friends and family.

Andrew and Jasmine spent all their waking hours together either in her room with Ashley or down the hall with Amy. The nurses in the medical/surgical unit teased Andrew, saying that if they wanted him for anything, they always knew where to find him—in the maternity ward!

Andrew noticed that Jasmine still battled with depression occasionally. Especially when she was alone and Ashley was asleep, Andrew would sometimes come in to find her staring out of the window with tears in her eyes.

But at least she was ready to talk about it now—with him—and with others as well. A counselor provided by the hospital had been in twice and Jasmine had also spoken at length with Pastor Thomas, who had flown down from Rabbit Lake to see them.

Pastor Thomas had told them that he'd also been to see Doctor Peters. Andrew and Jasmine were both relieved to hear that the judge had wasted no time in getting him sent to a treatment center. It was a private facility specifically designed for adult patients who were addicted to prescription drugs. It was recommended that family members refrain from visiting for the first two weeks, allowing for the drugs to leave the patient's system and for a treatment regimen to be instituted. Andrew was profoundly relieved to know that Jeff was not in a prison with hardened criminals but instead would finally be getting the help he needed. Jasmine had been very quiet as the pastor spoke and when he was done, she had whispered in a fragile voice, "I need help, too." Andrew had left them alone to talk then, taking baby Ashley with him down to the nursery so that he could spend time with Amy as well.

That had been on Tuesday. The pastor and Jasmine had talked again on Wednesday morning, this time at her request, with Andrew present. "Jasmine has taken the most difficult first step towards healing," Pastor Thomas said. "She is courageously facing the problem that she has been denying for so long."

"I was afraid to think about it," Jasmine confirmed. "I thought if I just forgot about the rape—but I'll never, ever forget it."

Andrew had Ashley in one arm. He gently took Jasmine's hand with his free one. She smiled gratefully up at him. "It's not so bad when you're not alone," she said.

"We're never alone," Pastor Thomas reminded her gently. "Sometimes it just feels that way. But we have only to reach out to Jesus and take hold of His hand…" He smiled. "…The way that you're taking hold of Andrew's. It takes courage to admit that we are weak—and that we need help—from God and from other people."

"I know that now," Jasmine said softly.

Chapter 14

ANDREW, JASMINE, AND ASHLEY could have been discharged on Wednesday, but they stayed one more day until the doctor felt confident about transferring Amy to the Rabbit Lake Health Center. Joshua had agreed to postpone the group meeting until Thursday night and Jasmine was thinking that it was just as well that they all had one more day before heading home. Andrew still looked a little pale and admitted that his leg still hurt, especially when he walked on it a lot. Although Andrew had accepted Colin's job offer, the doctor had advised him not to start his new job as a constable in Rabbit Lake for at least six weeks.

There was a big crowd out to welcome them home on the plane. Jasmine felt a little shy about it, but Andrew was almost bursting with pride as he showed off the two little girls and told everyone that Jasmine and he were engaged to be married.

Jamie and her two daughters, Rosalee and Kaitlyn, had spent the previous day giving the Peters' house a thorough cleaning. They'd made up both the beds in Jasmine's room, anticipating that Kaitlyn would stay with her until she got her full strength back. Of course, there were many other offers of help from the community ladies, both for meals and help with the twins.

Lewis Littledeer, Keegan's younger brother, had crafted two beautiful cradles for the babies. People in the community had "showered" Jasmine in her absence with many beautiful little outfits—some of them handmade. And there were sheets and diapers and lotions and powders... Missy itemized all the gifts as they were received so that Jasmine would know who they were from, but it was nice to have everything laid out and waiting when they arrived at the house.

Jasmine had no shortage of people who wanted to assist with their wedding, too. The only dark shadow was the thought that Doctor Peters might not be able to attend. Jasmine wanted to wait to set a date until they at least had some kind of an idea about when he might be released.

Andrew had spent almost every waking moment with Jasmine and the twins since they were born and he could hardly bear the thought of being in a different house from them now. Driving a car was still a little too much for him and it was too far for him to walk even the short distance between their two houses. They'd all gone directly to the Peters' house from the airport and Andrew's dad had said that he would come over and pick Andrew up whenever he was ready.

Sarah Hill delivered a supper meal to them and, after they'd eaten, Jasmine fed Ashley and left her in the care of Andrew and Kaitlyn while she went to the support group meeting. After a busy day of traveling and settling everyone in, Andrew had looked as if he would be better off going home to bed. But he'd told Jasmine that he wanted to be there for her when she came back from the meeting—in case she wanted to talk. And Kaitlyn had said that Andrew could just rest on the couch; she would do everything that needed to be done—cleaning up the dishes and taking care of the baby.

Jasmine was glad that Andrew would be waiting for her. She wished that he could go with her as well, but what she really wished was that she didn't have to go at all. But at the same time, she knew it was the right thing to do. It was like going to the dentist when you had a toothache. The process itself was painful, but not as bad as if the abscessed tooth was just left to get worse and worse.

Even though the distance was short between their two homes, Missy had picked up Jasmine and was planning to drop her off as well. It was still a bit early for her to be walking around a lot after her surgery.

The people assembled around a table up at the lodge seemed as nervous as Jasmine. Except perhaps for Joshua and Missy, who were taking the role of host and hostess, and facilitators for the group.

Each person was asked to introduce themselves. Joshua began. "Well, as all of you know, I'm Joshua and this is my wife Missy. We're expecting our first child on December 2." He paused a moment, looking around at everyone, a huge smile on his face. His announcement was met with applause and several congratulations. "I'm here tonight," he began in more somber tones, "both as a facilitator and as a participant." He took Missy's hand and his voice grew husky as he continued. "I don't want our child to have to go through what I did when I was young. I want to be a good father."

Joshua cleared his throat and went on. "Before we continue,

perhaps this would be a good time to draw your attention to the sheets in front of you. As you know, everything that we talk about around this table will be strictly confidential. I will ask you now to please sign these sheets. They state your willingness to commit to the full seven weeks and also your promise that everything spoken here will remain here."

There was some rustling of paper, followed by a time when no one spoke as they each read over what was written and then signed their names.

"You can just keep them with your materials," Joshua said. Then he turned to his wife and nodded.

She smiled. "Yeah, I'm Missy, and I guess I'm here tonight to learn and also to be a support to others. Joshua and I have gone through this program once and it really helped us in our relationship. As most of you know, I was completely blind all my life, until the operation, which was just eight months ago. I grew up in a world where I absolutely had to trust my family. Joshua grew up in a world where he couldn't trust his family at all." Missy turned towards her husband. "I think that's been one thing that we've struggled with."

Joshua agreed. "It's been hard for me just to rest in Missy's love. And sometimes I'm afraid to really let her know what I'm thinking and feeling."

They smiled fondly at each other. Then Joshua turned to the person on the other side of Missy. "Randi…"

The young woman had long black hair that she kept in a single braid down her back. She looked up nervously and then quickly back down again. "I—umm—I'm Randi." The young man beside her put his arm around her and she relaxed a little.

"I've been working with some of the staff sometimes during the day here at the camp. I did some cooking classes and one on childcare."

Joshua smiled in their direction. "Randi is also one of our best volleyball players. She was coaching the girls this past winter and got quite a good team together." Joshua nodded toward the next person. "Keegan…"

The young man had a regulation police haircut, his thick black hair spiked up a little on the top. He smiled around the table. "I'm Randi's husband. I guess most of you know." He looked over at Jasmine as he continued. Jasmine thought she was probably the only person who *didn't* know who everyone else was.

"We have one little boy named Chance," Keegan continued. "He's almost nine months old and crawling around, getting into all kinds of trouble and keeping his mom pretty busy. I'm a police officer here at Rabbit Lake and I would like to be able to understand and help the youth in the community. I grew up here and had my share of rough times." He put his arm around his wife again as he said, "We both did. I hope that we can learn and grow through this program, both individually and as a couple."

Keegan turned and grinned at the person beside him. "And this is my baby brother, Lewis."

He received a playful punch in the arm, which he quickly returned.

"Hey, hey, let's not have any of that," Joshua said with a laugh.

Lewis smiled good-naturedly. He wore his hair a little longer than his brother and was dressed in a more casual manner than

Keegan. He kept his eyes on his older brother, but his cheerful grin faded as he spoke seriously of their relationship. "Keegan and I did fight a lot when we were younger. But he also stuck up for me and he pulled me out of a lot of messes that I got myself into. He's been a really big support in the past few years, especially when—"

Everyone waited as he struggled for control. "My—my wife left me."

Jasmine looked away as tears filled Lewis' eyes. "It—it's not the first time." His voice trailed off into a whisper on the last word.

Joshua waited a moment before speaking. "We were hoping that Starla could join us for this session. When did you last hear from her, Lewis?"

The young man swiped at his tears and looked up. "Not since she left the camp. It's been about a month now." His voice became a dull monotone. "Someone said they saw her in Winnipeg just after she left here."

Joshua spoke in a sympathetic voice. "We'll be having a prayer time before we leave tonight. And we'll remember you through the week as well."

Others around the table nodded in agreement.

Jasmine knew that she was next. For a moment, her courage left her. But when Joshua smiled and introduced her as his "sweet, wonderful sister-in-law," she relaxed and began to speak. "First, I want to thank all of you for being willing to change the night for this meeting. I guess you know the reason I couldn't make it yesterday was because one of my twin babies wasn't ready to be discharged from the hospital. Actually, she was transferred to the Health Center here. Her name is Amy. Her older sister Ashley is home tonight with Kaitlyn and Andrew."

She smiled shyly. "Andrew and I are engaged to be married." There was a smattering of applause and congratulations from around the table in response to her statement.

Jasmine's smile gradually faded as she continued slowly, picking her words carefully as she went. "I became pregnant with the twin babies as a result of a rape that happened last summer. Because of—circumstances—I didn't work through that very well at the time. Through this past winter, I—got worse. I thought about death a lot. I thought about terminating the pregnancy. My father wasn't doing so well either. I—we—should have asked for help. I thought maybe it would all just go away. But then I knew that it wouldn't. It just—seemed to help—to not think about it."

Jasmine glanced at Joshua and Missy. Her older sister had tears in her eyes and Joshua didn't look too far from it.

Jasmine took a deep breath and continued. "Things came to a head a few days ago when my father was arrested for stealing drugs from the Health Centre. The next night, I knew that I couldn't go on. I took a knife—and tried to kill my babies. I thought that it would kill me, too."

Jasmine bowed her head in shame.

It was so quiet. Jasmine hazarded a glance up. But there was compassion in everyone's eyes—not condemnation.

She swallowed and forced herself to continue. There was more she had to say. "Andrew found me. He tried to stop me. We struggled with the knife. It was dark. I—I almost killed him." The enormity of what she had just said hit her then. What if Andrew *had* died?

"Jas…" Missy's gentle voice broke into the nightmare of her thoughts. "Andrew's okay."

"I—I know. It's just that—I could have—"

"But you didn't," Joshua said in a kind, firm voice.

Jasmine looked up, tears blurring her vision. "And the babies both lived, too. It was a miracle, but they're both okay."

"There were a lot of people praying," Keegan said.

Jasmine looked around at the assembled group. "I tried to ignore my problems and pretend that they didn't exist. I especially didn't want to talk about what happened to me—the rape. I just didn't think that it mattered anymore. But it did. I didn't want to be around people anymore. I did all kinds of things to help me forget—like overeating and watching too much TV. But in the end, none of it helped. I think that I was mad at God, too…" She looked over at Missy. "For taking our mother—and for what happened to me—and to our dad."

Her eyes moved from Missy to Joshua. "I want to face the truth now. I'm tired of running—and hiding. If this—what we're doing—will help me to do that—"

Joshua smiled reassuringly at her before addressing the rest of the group. "What Jasmine shared leads right into our topic for tonight. I hope that most of you have had a chance to look through the materials and through the readings in the text. We won't take a lot of time tonight to do that. Our evenings will mostly be a time when we can share together how the Lord has been working in our lives the previous week. The reading and homework/discussion questions should be done early on in the week so that you leave time for the Holy Spirit to effect healing in your life. Also, remember to pray for each other through the week. This is not an easy thing…" He smiled. "…But it is a good thing."

"Now, if you'll open your binders to Week One and read along with me: *The first step in our healing journey is to face the problem.*"

Joshua looked up as he continued to speak. "We need to look at the root cause of the things in our life that are out of control. Some of us have struggled with alcohol. Some with other illegal substances. Some with depression or anger or overeating. As you know, these things only temporarily dull the pain. Often we end up hurting other people—people that we love.

"When we hurt others and ourselves, we are also hurting God. The Bible teaches that we can 'grieve' or cause sorrow to the Holy Spirit by the way that we live. This, the Bible calls 'sin.' We can see the effects of that sin in our lives and in our families. We often focus on the outward behavior, such as alcoholism or drug abuse, but if we don't look at the underlying problems, we'll never get to the heart of the matter. We'll never really change.

"We need to ask God to show us the truth and we need to be willing to face that truth. Sometimes it's hard to admit to ourselves—and even harder to admit to others—that we have any problems at all. But it's important to allow God to show you those areas of your life that need change.

"If you have the answers to your homework/discussion questions ready…" Joshua looked over at Jasmine and smiled. "We'll excuse you for not doing your homework this week. Maybe you could just think about your answers as everyone else shares. And if you'd like to respond, we'll give you an opportunity for that as well."

Jasmine looked down at her assignment for the week:

1. What are the outward problems that I see in my life today? (Circle those which apply to you)

   Alcohol abuse, drug abuse, overeating, depression, suicidal thoughts, nightmares/night terrors, memory blocks, panic attacks, insomnia, addictive sex (pornography, promiscuity), gambling, compulsive TV or movie watching, compulsive shopping, workaholism, avoidance of people, lack of confidence, inability to make decisions, outbursts of anger, rage, abuse to others, loss of hope for the future, feeling distanced from God.

2. Ask the Holy Spirit to show you through the coming weeks what the root causes of these problems are.

Jasmine, looking through the list, could see that there were many outward problems that she could readily admit to. But, she wondered, how ready would she have been to look at these things a week ago? Not very ready, she had to admit. She'd had to be brought to a severe crisis in her life—a time when it was more than clear that she could no longer manage on her own.

As she listened to the others share, Jasmine silently thanked God for the way He had intervened in each of their lives. Not that all the struggles were over, but at least, for each one of them, the healing journey had begun.

As Missy drove her home, Jasmine reflected on how glad she was that she'd somehow found the courage to attend the first meeting.

From outside, Jasmine could see that the kitchen lights were off and she felt a twinge of disappointment. Perhaps Andrew had already left for home. She had hoped to talk to him, but knew realistically that he might be too tired tonight.

But they had a whole lifetime ahead of them...

Jasmine felt a surge of joy as she quietly opened the door and heard Andrew's voice softly singing. She glanced at a note left by Kaitlyn, saying she'd gone back home for a minute to get something.

Then all Jasmine's attention was on Andrew... sitting in an easy chair, holding Ashley gently in his arms, her head and shoulders resting in the palms of his hands. He was singing to her.

The low, sweet melody filled the room:

"Do you know that He cares for you, my little one?
Do you know He made each and every part of you?
Do you know He's planned your future?
One that's filled with hope, it's true.

Jesus made your eyes and eyebrows.
Made your hair and fingers too.
Made each little tiny footprint
Made each and every part of you.

Jesus is your Savior
Gave His life so you might know
That He loves all of His children
You and me and Mommy too."

As Andrew sang the last line, he was looking up at Jasmine. She laughed and walked into the living room.

"You just made that last part up," she said.

"Actually, I made the whole thing up," Andrew admitted with a wide grin.

He shifted Ashley so that she was cradled in his one arm and reached out with his other to take Jasmine's hand and draw her close.

"Hey, here's Mommy," he said as he pulled her onto his lap.

Andrew overruled her protests about weighing too much. "Just look at how beautiful she is," he said.

Jasmine replied, "Yes, she is."

And Andrew said, "I meant you."

Author's Note

If you have been sexually abused, it is very important that you talk to someone you trust: a teacher or your pastor or youth counselor.

If you know of someone under the age of fourteen who is being sexually abused, it is against the law to not report it to the authorities: the police or a social agency.

If you have been sexually abused in the past, the first step on your journey of healing will be to acknowledge that it happened and that it is affecting you today. You need to look honestly at the problems in your life and be willing to accept the help and counsel of others.

To know Jesus is to know the Great Healer. The Bible says that God loves you. He loves you so much that He sent Jesus to pay the price for your sin (it's like somebody taking your jail sentence for you so you can go free). Speaking of Himself in John 10:10-11, Jesus said: "I have come that they may have life, and have it to the full. I am the good shepherd. The good shepherd lays down his life for the sheep."

Jesus gave His life for you. But the Good News is that He didn't stay dead. He came alive again after three days. In doing so, Jesus conquered death forever.

To receive the free gift of eternal life, all we need to do is trust Him. A simple, but often difficult decision for someone who has been betrayed by those whom they should have been able to trust. Though your earthly father may have hurt you, your Heavenly Father loves you, and because He is perfect, His love for you is perfect.

Life here on earth may be difficult, but it is a journey we all must take. There is Someone who wants to walk beside us. When we talk to God and tell Him of our troubles, He hears us and the Bible says that the Holy Spirit is there to comfort us. As you read more of the Bible, you will learn more about God and He will speak truth to your mind and to your heart.

The Lord bless you!

M. Dorene Meyer

Recommended Resources

1. The Bible—available in many versions. Find one that's easy for you to read.
2. Visit www.risingabove.ca—excellent site that will direct you towards resources, conferences in your area, and hope and healing.
3. *Hope for the Hurting,* by Howard Jolly, published by Rising Above Counseling Agency in 1996.
4. *How to Counsel a Sexually Abused Person,* by Selma Poulin, also published by Rising Above Counseling Agency.
5. *Helping Victims of Sexual Abuse,* by Lynn Heitritter and Jeanette Vought, published by Bethany House Publishers in 1989.
6. *A Door of Hope,* by Jan Frank, published by Thomas Nelson Publishers in 1993.
7. *Breaking the Silence,* by Rose-Aimee Bordeleau, published by Raphah Worldwide Ministries in 2002, and available from www.raphah.org.

Questions for Group Discussion or Personal Reflection— Week One

1. What are the outward problems that I see in my life today? (Circle the ones that apply to you)

    Alcohol abuse, drug abuse, overeating, depression, suicidal thoughts, nightmares/night terrors, memory blocks, panic attacks, insomnia, addictive sex (pornography, promiscuity), gambling, compulsive TV or movie watching, compulsive shopping, workaholism, avoidance of people, lack of confidence, inability to make decisions, outbursts of anger, rage, abuse to others, loss of hope for the future, feeling distanced from God.

2. Ask the Holy Spirit to show you through the coming weeks what the root causes of these problems might be. Write down your thoughts as they come to your mind. Share them in support group or with someone else whom you can trust.

3. Write down or tell another person you trust about:
   a) an incident in your life when someone hurt you very deeply.
   b) talk (or write) about how you felt then.
   c) talk (or write) about how you feel about the incident now.
   d) talk (or write) about how the incident has affected your life—both then and now.

4. Write down or tell another person you trust about:
   a) an incident in your life when someone did something that made you feel loved.
   b) talk (or write) about how you felt then.
   c) talk (or write) about how this has affected your life—both then and now.

5. What are your feelings about God?
   a) Do you believe that He loves you?
   b) Has He ever shown you personally that He loves you?
   c) Do you believe that God is actively involved in your healing process?
   d) Draw a picture of yourself and God as you see your relationship with Him.